About

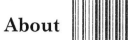

Sharon Keon was born in Hackney, East London and now lives in North London with her husband and two children. She enjoys knitting and crochet and updating her ever increasing bucket list, which included writing a book. Going to the cinema is a lifelong hobby, but she can usually be found in the kitchen trying out new recipes such as meatloaf cupcakes, as she has always enjoyed cooking. She recently combined this love of cooking with her love of travelling in a trip to Italy, which inspired *It Would Be Rude Not To*, her debut novel.

IT WOULD BE RUDE NOT TO

SHARON KEON

IT WOULD BE RUDE NOT TO

Vanguard Press

VANGUARD PAPERBACK

© Copyright 2021
Sharon Keon

The right of Sharon Keon to be identified as author of
this work has been asserted by her in accordance with the
Copyright, Designs and Patents Act 1988.

A CIP catalogue record for this title is
available from the British Library.

ISBN 978 1 80016 018 7

Vanguard Press is an imprint of
Pegasus Elliot MacKenzie Publishers Ltd.
www.pegasuspublishers.com

First Published in 2021

Vanguard Press
Sheraton House Castle Park
Cambridge England

Printed & Bound in Great Britain

Dedication

This book is dedicated to my first (but not my last) Italian cooking holiday on the Amalfi Coast. The people I met made the experience both memorable and enjoyable, and inspired me to write this book. Although the holiday and the people I met were real, the characters and their stories in this book are entirely fictional; however, some members of my cooking holiday group chose their character's name, so you know who you are!

Acknowledgements

Thank you to everyone on the trip, the travel company who organised everything brilliantly and were so helpful when things had to change. Thank you to Pegasus Publishers, who gave me the opportunity to tick off another thing on my bucket list. But most of all, thank you, Fleur, who believed I could do it.

Contents

Chapter One – Saturday: Getting There

Diana

Diana was five foot six, with dark brown hair that reached to the middle of her back (coloured to hide the grey), and blue eyes. Her eyes had recently been described as like 'looking into the world'; she had no idea what this meant and had not asked, instead she had taken it as a compliment.

When she was younger her hair had been blonde, like the girls you see on Bondi Beach, and with her blue eyes people had often described her as the 'milkman's daughter' as her family were all dark haired with brown eyes, her sister often mistaken for being Greek. This feeling of not belonging had stayed with her until the ripe old age of fifty-two. She had good skin, so she was told, few wrinkles and was reasonably slim, although the middle-aged spread was definitely something she wanted to work on, but she found it difficult to give up the bread, cheese and red wine, pasta, oh, and don't forget the chocolate.

Diana stopped on the other side of the ticket barrier, between the station and High Street Kensington. There was no going back now, not that she wanted to. Over the years her love of cooking had grown, from everyday meals to trying something different, like a spaghetti cake or meatloaf cupcakes and *The Naked Chef* had played a part (thank you, Jamie). She sometimes likened herself to a character from an old sitcom, where the mum proudly presented dishes to her family, sometimes standard, such as shepherd's pie or curry, and sometimes a little bit more themed, which were met with such comments as, "I'll try it, but don't be annoyed if I don't like it," and "Can we have fajitas or spaghetti bolognese tomorrow," not the only thing she had in common with sitcom Ria.

Today was a bucket list moment. Diana had for some time wanted to go on an Italian cooking holiday, relishing the thought of daily cooking lessons in a beautiful setting, with a group of likeminded people. She had decided that she would plan ahead for the year, making sure she had things to look forward to and something planned and exciting to do each month.

The thought of making real pasta and learning new recipes excited her—even on a normal day, she would wake up and immediately start to plan what to make for dinner that evening—so this holiday was going to be a real treat. Cooking was how she relaxed and she had come to rely on this time pottering in her kitchen. She found it de-stressing, therapeutic even, and it was also how she showed her family she loved them without actually having to say it.

She had found the holiday online and thought, *I'm doing it!* No more waiting for her grown up kids to decide if they wanted to go away with her, no more waiting for the husband to complain: he doesn't want to go here, the flight is too long, the plane seat is not big enough and incredibly, the beer is rubbish... She decided she was going to go and downloaded the information. She had happened to mention it to her cousin, Fleur, who also enjoyed cooking, and she had wanted to come along. She had booked the holiday for both of them and secretly been relieved. The thought of spending a week with strangers in a villa was both exciting and scary at the same time. What if they were loud or worse, boring? She did want an adventure for herself, after all.

Standing with her way too big purple case, which she had somehow managed to lug up the stairs—where was the escalator when she needed it—she took a breath. Here goes. She was meeting Fleur and travelling to Gatwick by taxi. They had been looking forward to this for months, but things had changed, and she would, after all, be spending the latter part of the week alone with a group of people she didn't know.

She was looking forward to a week where she could just be herself, do what she wanted, when she wanted, not be ruled by the clock; not having to get to work on time, not dropping off kids for their train on time. Not a mum, not a wife, not worrying about the kids and their problems. But she was nervous, too. She had never done anything like this before. She was often told she was a strong woman—"You're stronger than you think"—but the people who said that obviously didn't really know her, or perhaps couldn't be bothered to; they had their own lives after all.

She left the tube station and walked along High Street Kensington towards Holland Park. Turning left into the mews, she struggled to pull her new purple suitcase over the cobbles; she called Fleur to let her know she would be at the back gate in a few minutes.

Diana's themed Mexican evening

Cheesy nachos

Layer shop bought tortilla chips with lots and lots of grated cheese or thick slices of chilli flavoured cheese (or both) and warm in the oven. Once cheese has melted, top with sour cream, sliced jalapenos and serve. For extra special nachos, top with pulled pork or brisket.

Chicken Fajitas

Tortilla wraps, two per person, plus bowls of grated cheese, sour cream, guacamole and diced ripe tomatoes.

Marinade sliced chicken fillets, onions and peppers in a fajita sauce and cook on a very hot griddle.

Home-made fajita sauce

(After many experiments including with leftover Christmas turkey): half a teaspoon of paprika and cumin, 2 tablespoons of lime juice and olive oil, 2 garlic cloves, pinch of chilli, salt and pepper

.

Serve both with jugs of margarita and plenty of serviettes.

***

Fleur

Fleur looked at herself in the mirror. She was a good height, five foot seven, with good skin, light brown shoulder length hair and brown mischievous eyes. As she had got older—she was now fifty-six—everyone said she looked like her mum, who she missed dearly. She dressed in flowing tops and loose fitting, bright, sometimes referred to as a-bit-of-bling-clothes that she liked, whether they were from a charity shop or a high end designer. She was eclectic, well-travelled and had taken on the role of matriarch, regularly arranging and encouraging family reunions for all her cousins.

Fleur, aka Agnes. *What sort of parent would call their daughter Agnes in the late fifties*, she thought. It had been the time of rock and roll; the promise of new and exciting times ahead with the eve of the sexual revolution just around the corner. She should have been a Cindy, meaning moon, or a Tammy, meaning palm tree, anything but sounding like an old and ancient great aunt. And as far as she knew, there was no Aunt Agnes.

Her small cabin case was standing proudly in the corner of the room, ready to go, but she could not remember a thing she had packed, it was all a blur. Her year had started off in the usual way, but was now like the infamous 'annus horribilis'. So much had happened that she felt sort of numb. The sudden death of her husband had been bad enough, but then for that to be followed up with a diagnosis of breast cancer had been a terrible shock, one that felt surreal and like it was happening to someone else.

Looking at herself in the mirror, she thought, *I'm glad I decided to still go, even if it is only for a few days*. It wasn't perfect; she had so looked forward to a week learning to cook proper Italian food, like 'a nonna used to make', but at least a few days in Italy before major surgery would take her mind off things for a while. She hoped it would, anyway.

Her travelling inspired her cooking and she loved cooking recipes and dishes from her travels and entertaining large dinner parties, regaling them with her escapades, like her recent cruise where she had tried fried insects—not one for her dinner party, but who knows, Wholefoods may sell them soon—and there had been a curfew at ten p.m. as pirates could board the ship and kidnap tourists for a hefty ransom. She must write to the travel company as they had not told her that when she booked.

She also cooked the more traditional things for her local church events; her lemon loaf always went down well and was a favourite of her husbands, and who knew you could freeze lemon loaf, so batch baking wasn't a bad thing when she was bored.

Her mobile rang; Diana was here. Diana, a cousin she had not really spent much time alone with when they were both younger (why was that?), but as they had got older and found they had much in common, not only cooking, but life and outlook in general, they had grown closer. They understood some things about each other's lives, that others could not and often judged, voicing how they would have dealt with things differently. There was no judging, only friendly advice, sometimes not even that; they understood each dealt with things as best they could. They both got along and she was glad it was Diana this week. She did not want any stress or negative people around her; she wanted to forget, even if it was only for a few days. She let Diana in and they just had time for a cup of jasmine flower tea before the taxi arrived.

Fleur's Lemon Loaf

Beat 3 eggs, 6oz caster sugar and zest of 2 (most definitely) unwaxed lemons. Gradually add 6oz of plain flour, 1 teaspoon of salt, 1 teaspoon of baking powder; loosen mixture with 200ml of full fat milk and 1 teaspoon vanilla extract. Once all is mixed well, add softened butter. Pour into a greased 1lb loaf tin and bake in a low oven for approximately 80 minutes, but test the middle of the cake with cocktail stick before removing. If it comes out clean, it is ready. Leave cake in the tin to cool, but whilst still warm, prick all over with a cocktail stick and pour over lemon syrup topping.

Topping: heat 1.5oz of caster sugar and juice and zest of one large unwaxed lemon until reduced to consistency of syrup. Pour over loaf and leave to cool completely. Serve to church fête goers and husbands. Good for freezing if both cancel.

***

Anna

Anna was five foot one inch tall and she would describe herself as a little plump. She had short silver hair and bright blue twinkling eyes and at sixty-two felt as playful and rebellious as she did in her early teens. She always dressed in cool, flowing tops and linen trousers, her tops often embellished with Indian inspired embroidery.

Anna was looking forward to another Italian cookery holiday; this would be her third. She was hoping the group would be livelier than the last. She may be in her sixties, but she didn't feel it. She wanted to go dancing, to have fun, to meet new people, to drink limoncello on the balcony in the moonlight.

She had recently created a Facebook account, with the help of her daughter, and was slowly learning how to use it. She found it daunting, but brilliant at the same time. It was just wonderful how she could 'check in' and her daughter would like it and her son in Australia would comment. It made her feel closer to them somehow. Now she just had to work out how to post photos and not worry about the privacy settings, particularly as she had accidently posted a photo she would have preferred not to, her first selfie attempt which she felt had not been a pretty sight.

Anna was fiercely independent and had always been viewed as a bit of a rebel. She had gone to a good school, taken the eleven-plus and found grammar school easy. She was the only one in her family to go to university, a fight she had had with her mother, who had said it would be a waste of time as she would marry and stay at home and what would be the point. Surprisingly, her father had supported her. She wished he had been there when she graduated, but life was sometimes cruel and a heart attack had denied him, and her, this pleasure. She had gone into teaching and volunteered to teach overseas in India, which was where she had met Aksash. Aksash would have enjoyed this type of holiday, even though cooking was not his passion. He would have loved meeting new people and socialising over good home cooked food. His death had left a big hole in her life and for a while she had wondered what was the point, but a local cookery club had changed that. Her weekly get together had motivated her to book her first cooking holiday, and she knew this would not be her last. She closed the door and walked to the taxi. Next stop, Italy!

Anna's Carbonara

Mix 5 egg yolks with 5oz double cream and 3oz cheese (cheddar or parmesan, or more if you like). Fry or grill pancetta or smoked lardons and set aside on kitchen paper. Cook spaghetti or penne and drain, keeping just a splash of the cooking water. Put cooked pasta back in the pan (no heat), add the splash of cooking water to loosen, add the egg mixture, stirring quickly to prevent the eggs scrambling. Once all the spaghetti is covered, serve in warmed pasta bowls, top with the pancetta/lardons and sprigs of basil and drizzle of olive oil. Serve with a rocket salad and a good bottle of wine, with limoncello to follow, of course.

***

Francesca

Francesca was a tall, slim figure with reddish brown hair cut into a neat, professional bob. She dressed well and was in her forties with a good career and salary to match. Francesca wondered what on earth she had let herself in for? She had been bored one night and searching holidays online, she had come across a cooking holiday in Italy. Every year, she and her husband holidayed in Majorca, two weeks at the same five star hotel, where she spent the time relaxing and pampering herself in the spa. This would be followed by a holiday in the UK with her dogs, a trip she really enjoyed; the dogs were her babies after all. A sudden pang of guilt and feeling of loss stabbed at her; anyone looking at her would think she was about to burst into tears. She took a deep breath, pushed the thoughts to the back of her mind and thought, why not, it was about time she did something different and out of her comfort zone. She had clicked 'book online' and here she was, waiting at Naples airport for three other people she did not know, who she would accompany to the villa.

At forty-six, she felt restless. Her job in marketing took her many places, including Italy, but it was work after all. Her husband, Mark, had not wanted to come along. He was busy with his work and anyway, there were the dogs to look after. Once she had booked, she had instantly regretted being so rash. She enjoyed cooking, but it was not a passion. She had decided she would meet friends in Rome first and travel up to Naples by train the next day. If the week with a group of strangers proved awful, she could always go back to Rome.

Francesca's traditional shepherd's pie

Brown 1lb of minced lamb or beef, 1 diced onion, 2 medium diced carrots. Stir in 1 tablespoon of flour to coat all ingredients, then add 1 tablespoon of tomato puree (or ketchup if you have run out, or both) and 1 pint of beef stock (cubes okay). Simmer gently for approximately 20 minutes or until mixture thickens. Transfer to an ovenproof dish.

Cook 1lb of potatoes until very soft, drain and return to the pot. Add salt, pepper, splash of full fat milk and melted butter and mix well. Add onto the top of the cooked beef , sprinkle with cheese. Bake under a hot grill to brown and serve with crisp green beans or if no one is watching, baked beans and lots of ketchup.

***

David

David considered himself average height for a man, five foot ten; he had always wished he was taller. He was fortunate that in his late fifties he still had a slim build, given he liked his beer, and still had a good head of hair, albeit white. His blue eyes had often been described as piercing and his laugh annoying; the latter he agreed with and was constantly on guard after having heard himself in a video.

David wondered what on earth had possessed him to do this? He liked a barbecue and the odd dinner party, but was hardly MasterChef. His Malkin pie and Goosnargh cakes were renowned amongst his friends and family, but definitely local more than fine cuisine, and his social skills somewhat rusty outside his small circle of friends.

He had often thought of making a batch of pies and cakes and taking them along to one of the ever-increasing number of farmers markets that popped up at weekends and throughout the summer, but had not wanted to do this alone.

He had found himself alone unexpectedly later in life and did not like it. Since his divorce, he had met a few women, one in particular who he had really liked, Emma, and after one night and several messages he had mentioned going for a drink, but then he had not called her or made arrangements. To this day he was not sure why. They were still friends on Facebook; she often liked his photos and he hers, but that was that. Again, he was not sure why.

He had met his partner, Barbara, through a speed dating session ten years ago, an experience he never wanted to do again. He had gone along with a mate for a bit of a laugh, not knowing that most of the speed daters had done their research, looking up questions to ask and how to make yourself stand out and, most importantly, not look like a total loser.

He had arrived at the pub, to find some of his other mates there to watch the event and discover that he was totally unprepared. People were there on a mission, some to have fun, some to find a relationship and then there was him, Mr. Unprepared. He sat at the table and was relieved each time the pub bell was rung and they moved on. At fifty-nine, he was not ready for pipe and slippers but neither was he up for clubbing in Benidorm. He was a bit lost. The succession of tattooed, blonde, tanned ladies that sat opposite, waiting for his questions, was excruciating, made worse by the ever watchful eyes and the odd comment from his mates at the bar. Then Barbara had sat down, slim, bobbed brown hair, pale and patient and, most important, appearing normal. They talked briefly about cooking and running, the latter a passion of hers, and they clicked. It was easy and the past ten years had passed in a pattern of annual holidays, both together and apart, and three nights a week together, alternating between homes. Neither involved themselves in each other's extended families and they liked it this way.

He had parked at Manchester airport and flown to Naples, where he was collected and brought to the villa by taxi. Waiting on the terrace of the villa—he was the first to arrive—with a glass of prosecco, he thought about Barbara; she had not wanted to come to Italy, but come to think of it, had he actually asked her?

David's Malkin pie

Line pie dish with two thirds of shop bought shortcrust pastry. Layer up pie dish (found in charity shop) with seared lamb and beef chunks (bite size), braised sliced leeks, carrots, celery, onions, swede and smoked lardons.

Season each layer with salt and pepper.
Top with pastry lid and pierce to let the steam out.
Cook until you think it is ready.
Serve with a healthy helping of good friends!

***

Suzanne and Felipe

Suzanne was very slim, something she was proud of, as she exercised regularly and watched her weight and calorie intake. She dressed casually, having little time for fancy dresses or outfits, or people that wore fancy dresses, and had a dark brown pixie cut hairstyle that was easy to maintain and suited her petite face.

Suzanne had turned sixty the previous year, and to celebrate her husband, Felipe, had planned and taken her on a trip of a lifetime to South America. They had done all the usual touristy things—visited Machu Picchu and Christ the Redeemer, dined on Copacabana Beach and eaten steak and empanadas in Buenos Aires—but this was the holiday that was on her bucket list. She loved Italian cooking, although Felipe had taken over the kitchen now, given he was retired.

They enjoyed their life in Guernsey; they had a lovely home, outdoor area with a pizza oven and entertained friends and family regularly. Their son had recently opened a small café and they often helped with event catering, preparing and serving giant seafood paellas. She looked at her phone and checked the number of steps she had walked today; she must ensure they kept their routine on this holiday.

Felipe was sixty-five with a full head of fair hair, hazel eyes and a slimmer build than at the start of the year, thanks to Suzanne. He watched Suzanne checking her step counter again. This was not a trip he would have booked; he preferred sightseeing or beach or a bit of both, but never say never had become his motto.

Retirement had come as a bit of a shock initially, but he was now getting into it. Retiring from a large company as a managing director had been very daunting. However, having time to play golf when he wanted, being able to lay in, not having to clock watch, no meetings and no awkward people to manage was nice. It had taken time for him to relax and he often felt there was a whole new sub culture of older people, doing what they wanted, when they wanted, without any younger people to interfere with their younger people's ways. The only problem was Suzanne. She still worked. She enjoyed her job in the local school and did not want to stop. He often asked her why, they didn't need the money, his savings and pension provided more than a comfortable life. He was hoping the promise of more holidays like this would persuade her.

Felipe had booked them a night in Naples, where they had visited Pompeii and Herculaneum, and they had then travelled to Positano for one night and then caught the water taxi to the villa, arriving at the jetty by the small pool, filled with seawater, like film stars, or at least VIPs. The flight of steps up to the top terrace looked intimidating, but the sea looked very inviting. Swimming here daily would satisfy Suzanne's' step counter, meaning he could indulge in the odd beer or two in the evening.

Felipe insisted on travelling light with only a rucksack each; he hated the queues at check in and baggage collection, with people taking too long, whereas he would be in and out in a flash, why was that? On this occasion, the rucksacks had been the right decision, there was no way he would get a suitcase let alone two, up those rocky stairs.

Suzanne and Felipe's Paella

Purchase authentic paella pan from the internet or better still, bring one back from your travels. Heat 1 tablespoon of olive oil in a pan and sauté 1 diced onion until soft. Add 300g of paella rice and stir in 1 teaspoon of paprika and 50ml of white wine. Once reduced, add 1 pint of chicken stock and 1 tin of chopped tomatoes. Simmer until the liquid has reduced and rice is almost tender. Add sliced chorizo (£1 coin size) and cooked prawns (shell on). Cook for a further five minutes to ensure chorizo and prawns are warmed through. Remove from heat, squeeze lemon juice over and sprinkle liberally with torn up flat leaf parsley and lemon wedges. Serve with a smile and crusty bread bought from the local artisan bakery. Sangria optional.

***

Gianluca

Gianluca was Sicilian, five foot eight, slender, toned and olive skinned with deep brown eyes and a voice that was soft and lilting. He knew he was a catch, but he had not met the right Italian, Sicilian girl yet.

Gianluca sighed, another week of strangers wanting to learn to cook 'proper Italian' food was about to begin. He would host and help the chef prepare the lessons and meals and regale the group with tales of his exploits in Antarctica. Everyone loved those stories and photos.

David was already here, meeting Suzanne and Felipe who had just arrived at the jetty. Fleur (interesting name), Diana, Anna and Francesca were on their way with Giovanni, the taxi driver. *Let's hope they make it in one piece*, he thought, thinking only briefly of Giovanni's driving. Gianluca was also hoping that the four women would be good company and not look at him as a potential holiday romance. He was not interested; he had a career and a future to plan.

He was well travelled, including time as a private chef to a Russian oligarch on his super yacht. He had spent two years travelling the world on the yacht, mostly by himself with a small crew, which had been a great experience. However, when the call came and the helicopter was landing with the Russian and his entourage, the yacht became a very different animal. He was on call twenty four hours, as was every other member of the crew. What the Oligarch wanted, the Oligarch got. Sometimes the bodyguards stayed briefly on board whilst the Russian went ashore and he remembered one time being told in no uncertain terms to do as he was told as they had their way of dealing with things, which he took to mean he could be dining with the fishes if he wasn't careful.

Following his time with the Russians, he had spent time in London, Paris and South America and lastly, a year in the Antarctic for a NASA research project, before returning to act again as host for Italian cookery holidays. He had met many women along the way, but none that he had wanted to settle down with. He had decided this would be his last year of travelling. Later this year he would be going home to Sicily to find a wife.

Gianluca's Russian Blinis

Sift 2oz of buckwheat flour with 6oz of plain flour and 1 teaspoon of salt. Add one sachet of dried yeast. Loosen 8oz crème fraiche with 8oz full fat milk and warm gently. Separate 2 eggs and whisk yolks, adding to the flour mixture. Once everything is mixed together, cover and leave in a warm place (i.e. next to oven). Meanwhile whisk egg whites and then gently fold into the mixture, leave for another hour. Melt butter in a nonstick pan and add 1 teaspoon of mixture per blini. Flip when firm and golden brown, remove from pan and leave to cool.

Ensure blinis are perfect bitesize rounds, topped with piped whipped crème fraiche and beluga caviar (shipped from Fortnum and Mason). Serve as a canape to Russian Oligarch and hope the bodyguards approve.

***

Rocco

Rocco was in his forties and an experienced chef with a published cookbook. *Annoying that the travel company would not allow him to sell his books*, he thought. He spent his days in chefs' whites and crocs and enjoyed cooking and teaching others how to cook. His brown curly hair was greying, but he felt he looked distinguished, a short Italian George Clooney perhaps? He kept himself trim and enjoyed the company of women (although not so much these days). His brown twinkly eyes and softly spoken Italian had got him into trouble before.

Rocco thought, *Another day, another Euro. Mamma mia, here he goes again, another cooking holiday for a group of people from across the world (this time England) professing to be interested in learning to cook real Italian recipes.* He hoped they would not ask for certain dishes; he had a routine, a budget and limited nearby shopping facilities, the nearest market being a thirty minute drive away. He was also discovering the villa was not exactly stocked with the latest gadgets; he was having a hard time finding a vegetable peeler, let alone a potato ricer. The small kitchen was rammed with a lot of lovely expensive crockery from the local area; decorated with lemons and very brightly coloured, but there was not a decent wine glass to be found.

At forty-three, he was not married, but had a partner and young child. He had promised his partner she had nothing to worry about, he was committed to her and their child and anyway, since the last time, he had learnt his lesson, no more holiday liaisons, one near miss with a bunny-boiler was enough. Social media, Mamma mia, it made it very easy for past lovers to find someone, track their whereabouts and their friends.

Rocco thought of Gianluca; he had worked with him before and thought they were a good team. He was the mature, distinguished, volatile chef, whilst Gianluca was the younger, calmer, good looking one. He was trying to persuade Gianluca to be a partnership and work towards a career in the media. After all, if the 'two greedy Italians' got a series, why couldn't they?

He would get ready, put on his chefs' whites and begin to prepare the evening meal in the tiny kitchen; how he was going to teach there he had not quite worked out. He hoped the group would all be here on time and he would not have to serve dinner late; he liked things organised and on time. Plus, there was also football on the TV later.

**

Chris

Chris looked at his phone, waiting for a message sent from the other side of the world. Chris was heading toward the big four-o. He had short, spiky hair that used to be light brown, but was definitely now a peppered variety of greys, and pale blue eyes. He always had stubble and was of a stocky build, having played semi-professional rugby in Australia and Europe for several years. His travels had taken him to many places and that was how he had come to meet her, when he had worked briefly as a supply teacher. Chris looked forward to the photos he would receive with the usual message—'wish you were here, gorgeous'—and he nearly always responded with 'hey, hot stuff'. He too wished he was there instead of at home in Australia.

For years they had been in contact through social media, but they had not met again since his return to Australia all those years ago. Life had been unexpectedly challenging for him: illness, divorce and now a single father, at nearly forty, it was not how he had envisaged his life would be. She spoke little about her life and he did the same. They were happy to have a bit of banter and think what if and what could possibly be.

He remembered her, the older woman. He had been twenty-nine, she was about forty. It had surprised him that he had even wanted an older woman; but he had always liked women and them. He seemed to like women who were different, something he had told her, and thought immediately that he shouldn't have.

He had started work at the school as a supply PE teacher and had noticed her in the office, when the receptionist, a very mature lady with obviously dyed jet black hair, a very wrinkly (smoker's) face, he thought, and a twinkle in her eye, had greeted him with, "Hey, good looking." She had looked up, caught his eyes and turned away immediately, blushing. He had thought at that time, it would be easy to seduce an older woman, but she had laughed at his every chat up line and turned down his invites to nights out in London at typical Aussie hangouts. He knew she had wanted to go, that she was tempted, but he had not known until he returned home how much she had struggled with her decision to be a good wife, a good mother.

He remembered the chats in her office, where they talked so easily about movies and music, where they had holidayed and where they would like to travel to next. But he knew she had talked about anything to avoid the tension; he remembered he had wanted to sweep the desk of paper, and pens, all the office paraphernalia; just sweep it all on the floor; pull her on the desk and have sex there and then. He remembered her going red when a colleague had laughingly said, "For god's sake, you two, just get it over with, you could cut the sexual tension in here with a knife." He had known she had wanted that too, deep down.

He thought of the times she had asked for his help, seeking him out to do little jobs for her, excuses like she needed help carrying boxes to a cupboard; a dim secluded room where he had imagined more than once shutting the door and pushing her against it; lifting her dress, kissing her; but he had not, he had known then he wanted to make love to this woman. There was something different about her.

He had been sad not to see her on his last day at school before he flew home; it was not what he had planned as he was sure there would have been a snog in it somewhere, but it had not worked out that way. Although he had desperately wanted to see her one last time, a bad hangover from the night before had meant he had slept in. When he woke, he woke feeling a sense of loss, not only as he would not see her again, but also he had left his favourite pencil case in class, one that had been with him since teacher training.

He had emailed from the airport on his way home to say he was sorry to have missed her and later had sent a friend request through Facebook. He had been surprised when she had accepted him almost immediately, and even more surprised and touched when she had forwarded his pencil case, filled with little red hearts (postage must have cost her a bit). His mum, on the other hand, was not impressed, as glittery little red hearts had covered her kitchen table and were found in odd places for months after.

Over the years they had kept in touch and although she did not know this, her messages, chats and photos had kept him going through some very dark times. He had begun to look forward to them, enjoying the banter, particularly the chats about that one night out he had arranged through mutual friends. They had all met up at a local restaurant, after the girls had eaten, as he could not afford a meal; She had just got dessert when he arrived and they shared it. The group had moved upstairs to the club, where he had tried to kiss her and she had just said, "Shut up and dance with me." Her friends at the time had been aware she was tempted and looked out for her, he was still not sure it had been the right decision.

He wanted to see her, wanted to hold her, all these years of keeping in contact had to mean something. Perhaps he should just jump on a plane and head to the Amalfi Coast and finally get the 'what ifs' over and done with.

Chapter Two – First Evening

Gianluca rolled his eyes, already a drama. David had slipped on the jetty steps whilst meeting Suzanne and Felipe, and fallen awkwardly, hurting his shoulder. Gianluca was sure he required hospital treatment, but David was adamant. He wanted it strapped up and he would see how he felt in the morning.

Gianluca took another bottle of prosecco to the terrace for Suzanne and Felipe, and water and painkillers for David. already had a feeling his budget would be tested this week. He could hear Rocco mumbling in the kitchen, lamenting that the others were late, that dinner would be spoilt, that he would miss his football later, but he had spoken to Giovanni; they would be here very soon.

Gianluca left the three guests on the terrace and made his way up the rocky steps to the top of the villa, and opened the electric gates with a gadget he carried at all times. The minibus would be here imminently and he could not afford to block traffic at night on this coast road. Only last week there had been a fatal moped accident, someone he thought Rocco might know, but he wasn't sure. Rocco had not said so and if anything seemed to avoid talking about it.

Anna, Francesca, Diana and Fleur were busy hoping they would make it to the villa in one piece. Since being picked up at Naples airport by Giovanni, they had sped through traffic, horn honking, and at times with their eyes shut; not Giovanni, though, they hoped. Giovanni had spent most of the journey on his mobile phone, stopping his call only briefly to point out the dark and brooding Vesuvius to the left.

He drove the taxi with one hand, which had been bearable on the roads out of Naples, but breathtakingly scary along the Amalfi coast road in near darkness, the sea and sheer drop on one side and rising ominous cliffs on the other. At one point, Anna had gripped Diana's hand and said in a rather loud, high voice, "Driving is certainly an adventure here in Italy; let's hope we live to tell the tale."

On and on the coast road went, and Diana made a mental note to check transfer times much more thoroughly in future when she booked any trip. The twinkling lights of the houses on the cliff sides and boats out at sea were beautiful, and made the drive along the coast road somehow less threatening; Diana made up stories to herself about the people she saw after catching glimpses of couples as they passed restaurants, and the warm breeze coming in through the open driver's window, together with snatches of Italian music and the scent of lemons growing by the roadside, was intoxicating.

Arriving at the villa, Giovanni navigated the minibus off the coast road and through the already open gates, dim lights waiting to welcome them into the small area in which to park. He jumped out and opened the sliding door, still on his mobile and beckoned the four women out. The area was surrounded by bougainvillea with worrying stone steps leading down to what Diana assumed was the main villa, bedrooms and other terraces.

Giovanni retrieved the suitcases from the back of the minibus and deposited them on the terrace. Gianluca introduced himself to the four women, explaining they would be joining the others shortly.

Diana spotted a small chair pulley and although it looked very scary, with only a small scaffold looking type chair, she was first to go towards it and attempt to sit down. Gianluca hurried over; it was for the suitcases, not people he explained, grinning. Diana, bit her lip sheepishly, chiding herself once again not to assume anything; this reminded her of the time she had sat down and poured herself a glass of water in a restaurant, only for the waiter to come over and put tea lights in the other 'glasses' whilst looking at her pityingly, or the time she had ordered ribs for the first time and was about to drink the lemon water, until the waiter had pointed out with disdain that this was for her to freshen her hands. She should remember by now to never assume anything, ask if in doubt. She remembered a saying, 'don't make an ass out of u and me'; a saying that she disliked, probably because a particularly horrible, thankfully now ex-colleague used to quote frequently.

With Gianluca in the lead, the four women headed down the many rocky steps, visibly hewn from the cliffs; steps that were fortunately quite wide as it took two strides to get to the next step. On the way down they were allocated bedrooms; Francesca at first stop down, Anna, Fleur and Diana another flight down. Fleur had been allocated the best room (it was only right), with a balcony overlooking the sea. Diana looked forward to coffees on that balcony in the morning and a nightcap in the evening. Anna was in the room to the right of Fleur, Diana was opposite Anna. Diana immediately nicknamed her room the cave. It was dark, very traditionally old Italian and two walls, one in the bedroom and one in the bathroom, had part of the cliff exposed. She hoped both walls had been thoroughly cleaned and there was absolutely no trace of a creature of any sort.

Diana opened her suitcase and put a few things out, changed her shoes and top and freshened up a little. She grabbed a small bag for keys and phone and knocked for Fleur. They joined the rest of the group on the upper terrace, by two internal staircases. Not knowing the way, they followed the laughter to find the group enjoying prosecco on a terrace which had fantastic views of Amalfi.

Diana thought Gianluca looked worried as he brought another bottle out. The newcomers asked David what he had done to his shoulder and questioned whether he should drink, given Gianluca had provided painkillers. David's shoulder did not look good and seemed to be drooping. Apart from David, the group all thought he would be spending time in an Italian hospital tomorrow.

Rocco announced dinner was served and they all sat down to dishes of salad, bread, meatballs and spaghetti. The conversation flowed easily, as did the local wine, with everyone introducing themselves and describing a little about themselves, their families and where they were from. Gianluca asked if the group would like another bottle of prosecco and Felipe said, "It would be rude not to," a phrase that would become associated with Felipe and the holiday as a whole.

Diana felt relieved; perhaps this week would be better than she had hoped.

Chapter Three –Sunday: the First Cooking Lesson

Diana awoke early as usual, why was it she couldn't have a lie in anymore? Apart from feeling like her body was on automatic pilot; she found it hard to relax. Years of being ruled by the clock, must be at school on time, then get to work on time, then leave on time to collect the children, take them to clubs, pick up from clubs, music lessons and so on had resulted in this groundhog day status; when would it change, would it change? She often wondered if everyone else talked to themselves as much as she did.

Diana opened the window and the light streamed into the dark room, exposing the cliff wall behind her bed in all its glory. Her window looked out onto a terrace full of bougainvillea, framing the panoramic views of the sea and cliffs of the Amalfi Coast,

Diana got ready and went for a stroll around the villa, rumoured to be worth twenty-one million euros (one of last night's conversations).

The villa was spread over several levels, the various bedrooms and lounges reached by stairs inside and rocky steps and curving stairways outside the villa, both of which were steep and a just a little bit of a worry. One room would lead to another room and terrace and then another and so on. The villa was a wonder of sprawling rooms, terraces and spectacular views, all of which were breath-taking, and Diana felt she would never find her way around, even after a week.

After making a mental note to not wear any heels in order to get up and down the stairs and steps without breaking her leg or something worse and then asking herself, *How old are you*, at the same time, Diana surveyed the interiors. Although there was little evidence of being in the twenty-first century, apart from Wi-Fi (thank goodness) and one big TV, the villa was stunning.

Rooms had ceramic tiled floors, with large inserted tiled borders, the colours of which were matched in the dado and picture rails. In one room, Diana was strangely reminded of the old pie and mash shop that her mum had taken her to most Saturdays when visiting her gran in East London, which had also had green and white tiles on the floor and walls. *No sawdust here, though*, she thought and smiled to herself whilst moving on to the next room.

There were chandeliers and soft white drapes at each window and door, and eclectic sofas, all in different fabrics and patterns, but complementing each other in soft gold, cream and terracotta. Ginormous white and gilt urns and vases on pedestals were tucked away in corners, some holding floral arrangements, which appeared effortless, but had probably taken someone with skill some time to arrange.

Another room had a magnificent ceramic tiled mural insert in the floor, blue and yellow in design, and incorporating lemons, a fruit she had found out last night, was synonymous with the Amalfi Coast and had its own department dedicated to the protection of the lemon (according to Rocco). The mural had a large highly polished wooden table stood upon it with a chandelier hovering above it. The table was adorned with a huge bowl of fruit (Diana took a few grapes to nibble) and a variety of glass and silverware. Looking around the room, with all its ornaments and trinkets, Diana wondered if the owners lost more than the odd bath towel here.

The views from the terraces were spectacular and she could imagine movie stars from the '60s and '70s lounging around the grand rooms and terraces, having fabulously lavish parties with PAs and butlers running around after them and paparazzi staked out on the cliffs above and out to sea, hoping to get a photo that would earn them notoriety as well as the cash. According to Gianluca, the villa of a famous Hollywood actress was just along the coast road and was also available to rent at a mere four thousand euros per night. Diana wondered what the villa had to justify that price tag; she would expect the Hollywood actress as host for that amount, she giggled to herself.

Going out onto one of the terraces, Diana looked over the balcony with a turquoise railing to another terrace below and one above. Each terrace was paved with large terracotta tiles and a variety of chairs, tables and loungers lay around waiting to be used. The balcony was festooned with terracotta pots of wild flowers lining the length of the terraces and Diana wondered where the gardener was who maintained them.

Diana had taken numerous photos and sat down on one of the many chairs on the terrace to edit and post them. She enjoyed sharing photos and experiences with friends and family; when they commented or just 'liked' it, it made her feel like they were thinking of her, cared even. Some people often ridiculed her like of Facebook, but she ignored them; it had been her lifeline on many occasions, a link to extended family; plus she felt they were trying to manipulate her into their way of thinking, something she had put up with for far too long.

Diana made her way to a small winding staircase, where the treads were wooden and the risers tiled with a floral pattern. She found it quite hard as the right handrail was draped with a garland of ivy, so she had to go up on the left-hand side.

Diana made her way to the kitchen and met Gianluca, who was getting breakfast ready. She could tell they would get on; he was easy going and

47

considering he was twenty odd years younger, he was very at ease with older people and made her feel comfortable. He was a good host. Gianluca made a pot of coffee and she took this off to Fleur's room to show her the photos she had taken.

Fleur woke with a start, where was she? She looked around the unfamiliar surroundings and slowly remembered. She got up, opened the balcony doors and went to shower. The bathroom had long windows opening out to sea, no blinds. *Oh well*, she thought, no one was going to see her naked other than a passing seagull.

Whilst towel drying her hair, she caught sight of herself in the mirror. She would look different in a few days. She had always liked her big boobs, but she was weirdly looking forward to having smaller, new, perky boobs. Strange how things worked out; her late husband had been tall and lean and had grown more handsome as he had aged, he would have liked the smaller, perkier boobs too.

Fleur heard a knock at the door and Diana called to say she had coffee for the balcony. Standing looking out to sea with Diana, she watched the small fishing boats and yachts go by, ferries further out, whilst drinking the strongest coffee she had ever tasted. The views were one of the most beautiful she had ever seen, but wonderfully understated and calming.

Diana pointed excitedly to something out to sea, a school of dolphins swimming by. They could not believe it, about ten dolphins, all different sizes, just jumping up and down in the sea and swimming on, following a small boat, presumably a fishing boat. Fleur thought, she had paid good money to see this on previous holidays to Florida and the Caribbean, expensive boat trips for her and the kids to see dolphins in the wild, but trips she felt sure were set up, contrived even. Yet here they were, dolphins going about their daily business, no tourists, no boat trips bribing them with titbits; oblivious to the amazed bystanders on the balcony of a nearby villa on the Amalfi Coast.

Their excitement caused heads to pop out of the bedroom window next door. Suzanne and Felipe climbed out of their window and joined them, marvelling at the dolphins, such a wonderfully natural sight; what a treat; although Diana thought she saw Suzanne look enviously at the balcony door. This holiday was going to be full of surprises.

Their breakfast, although minimal—no full English here—was tasty enough. Lots of fresh bread, toast, cereal, freshly squeezed juices, including blood orange, and pots of tea and coffee. Best of all, Diana thought, was the lemon marmalade, although as Gianluca had pointed out that it cost seven euros a jar, she hoped it would last the week; she guessed he had a budget to stick to. Their first cooking lesson was at ten a.m., and they were all looking forward to it, apart from David. Gianluca had arranged transport to take him to the local hospital.

The small group assembled on the terrace outside the kitchen. The large table where they had eaten dinner alfresco the evening before, had been set up with pasta boards topped with a recipe sheet and a large knife. Ingredients were in blue and white bowls and plates, laid out down the middle of the table. Diana looked around and thought she could not have imagined this setting if she had tried. Cooking on a terrace with views out to sea and the sun shining, she was so glad to be here.

They were to make pasta, tagliatelle to be exact, which they would have for lunch. Everyone donned their holiday apron embellished with the holiday company logo and waited for Rocco, who they could hear in the kitchen, grumbling about the lack of utensils. He came out brandishing a roll of cling film, complaining, "Mamma mia," there was no way to tear off strips and what sort of kitchen was this? Diana looked around the small group; she wondered if she was the most eager to learn. This was the lesson she was most looking forward to.

First Cooking Lesson -Two Types of Tagliatelle

Lemon Pasta with Prawns and Basil Pasta with Mozzarella and Tomatoes

2 cups 00 flour
2oz finely chopped basil or zest and juice of one large lemon
2 eggs
1 tsp salt
1 tsp olive oil
Prawns
Cherry tomatoes
Mozzarella balls

Rocco allocated jobs: Diana to finely chop the basil, Felipe to zest the lemons, Fleur to put two cups of flour onto each of the pasta boards, Anna allotted the eggs, and Francesca measured the salt and oil.

Rocco made a well in the centre of his flour and cracked in the eggs, salt and oil. He then added some of the lemon zest and juice, explaining the group could choose to make either the lemon or basil pasta. Rocco then gently and slowly whisked the wet ingredients with a fork and then began to gradually pull in the flour from the outside edges, mixing until everything was worked together. Rocco worked gently with the sticky mixture until a soft dough was formed.

The group began to follow the demonstration, laughing and taking photos along the way. When they had all reached the dough stage, Rocco extolled the 'need to knead' and how important it was to use the heel of your palm to gently push and roll the dough out, turning and kneading until the imprint of a finger returned the dough to its rightful shape. The doughs were then covered with cling film and left to rest on the corners of the pasta boards, laying in the sun like relaxed sunbathers.

Each of the guests took a handful of the reddest tomatoes Diana had even seen from one of the blue and white bowls on the table and cut them in half, returning them to the bowl when cut. To the kitchen now, Rocco beckoned, picking up the bowl of tomatoes and explaining the prawns were waiting.

Diana looked around the small kitchen, much too small for the size of the villa she thought, and understood why Rocco was grumbling so much now. The kitchen was quaint, eclectic and not in the least modern. It was cramped and there were no sleek units or high tech ovens or equipment here. Instead a mishmash of units, open shelving and an island in the middle, which somehow included the oven, hob and sink. Above the island there was a shelf, suspended from the ceiling, loaded with plates, pots, pans and utensils and the walls and floor were a hectic display of patterned baroque tiles. There were two doorways into the small kitchen, one with a brick archway leading to the dining terrace; to the right of the sink was an old wooden table, under which boxes were stacked and covered with a blanket. *Gianluca's secret stash of wine and prosecco*, thought Diana, *not so secret now*. The only nod to modernity was the large American style fridge freezer, which looked completely out of place.

In the kitchen, Rocco retrieved a bowl of large, plump, grey prawns from the fridge, after shooing Francesca out of the way of the door, and set them to one side. The halved tomatoes were placed in a sieve over a bowl with a little salt and he did both tasks while complaining to himself and anyone listening about the size of the kitchen and how could he possibly teach in it.

Rocco picked up a prawn and demonstrated separating the head from the body and peeling away the outer shell and then, using a small sharp knife, cutting along the back of the prawn to remove the stringy vein. Diana was not sure about the latter task; she adored prawns and had peeled and eaten them since a child, but removing the vein looked stomach churning! She remembered Sunday night teas with her mum, when the winkle man turned up in his van, like the ice cream man but with a bell not the music. She would run outside with a tin mug and ask for a pint of prawns and a pint of winkles, which would be their tea with bread and butter. She was nudged sharply back to this century and reality by Felipe, who told her to stop daydreaming. One by one, they all took turns to remove the vein or intestinal tract, Felipe happily pointed out, when it was Diana's turn, until all the prawns were ready to cook.

Leaving the small kitchen, the group returned to their doughs. The cling film was removed, and each rolled the dough out to a thin, long oval. Everyone concentrated on rolling and turning the dough, sprinkling the board and the rolling pins with a little extra 00 flour to prevent any sticking. When the thin oval shape was achieved, almost covering the entire pasta board, strips were then cut, about one centimetre in width, to form the Tagliatelle strips. Boards were piled high with delicate lemon or basil pasta ribbons, which were gently trickled into nests and set aside, ready to cook for lunch later.

Gianluca announced it was time for a break and brought out a tray of pretty flute glasses filled with prosecco and Diana could see the bubbles fizzing in the glasses, dancing and popping in the sunshine. Suzanne and Felipe busied themselves taking photos on their iPad, whilst Fleur and Diana posted photos for their family and friends to see. Anna sat on the terrace admiring the beautiful Amalfi coastline, enjoying the company and fizzy sensation from the prosecco, whilst Francesca joined Rocco in the kitchen.

Two bottles of Prosecco later, the group reconvened in the small kitchen where Rocco had a pan of melted butter, garlic and olive oil gently sizzling on the small hob. Two pots of steaming water were also on the cramped hob, patiently awaiting the pasta, which Rocco said would take only minutes to cook as it was so fresh. As space was tight, Rocco explained he would demonstrate each pasta dish for the group to sample and then he would prepare lunch for the group alone. *Mamma mia*, Rocco thought. He was not sure how he was going to cook for the whole week in this tiny kitchen; thank god it was a small group.

Rocco added prawns to the melted butter and garlic together with a glass of white wine. In another pan on the side, the tomatoes were covered up to keep warm. A handful of each freshly made tagliatelle was added to the boiling water in each of the two pans. The prawns were tossed and removed quickly when they were pink and juicy, just a few minutes. A sprinkling of the 00 flour was added to the liquid to thicken it. The pasta was removed and placed in two of the many rustic but decorative bowls of the region that the kitchen cupboards and shelves were stacked with. The basil pasta was tossed with torn mozzarella, warmed tomatoes and drizzled with olive oil; the lemon pasta with prawns and the thickened sauce, and topped with chopped basil and a hint of lemon zest.

The first lesson ended with cheers of delight as they tasted the dishes, each sure it was the best pasta they had ever tasted. Rocco then ushered the group out of the kitchen with a few grumbles and told them lunch would be served shortly on the terrace, if he could manage it in such a small space. Diana could hear Rocco continue to grumble to himself as she left the kitchen and was sure she also heard Gianluca say he would have to negotiate a discount with his wine guy as he would need to buy in bulk for this week.

Chapter Four – Free Afternoon then Dinner

Lunch was a very relaxed affair. Everyone enjoyed the food they had made and Rocco had finished preparing, all served with copious amounts of prosecco.

David returned from hospital during lunch with his arm and shoulder strapped very tightly to his chest and he explained he had strict instructions for it to remain this way for at least twenty-four hours. He had broken his shoulder, but had decided to stay the week in the villa anyway. Diana wondered how he would cope, but then watching Gianluca, who was already taking care of him, she also wondered how Gianluca would feel after a week; after all, David would need a lot of help, even with dressing.

After lunch Diana and Fleur changed into their swimwear, gathered their things and met on the terrace outside Diana's bedroom. They made the treacherous walk down to the small pool area which overlooked the sea, via the steep narrow steps carved out of the cliff side, with only a loose rope bannister to hold on to. The rocky terrace with the sea water pool was also carved from the cliffs, with a few more steps and a small landing into the choppy sea. *This must be where David fell*, Diana thought.

Sun loungers meant they could laze, looking out to sea and the Amalfi coast line, dotted with cliff edge villas until the cliffs disappeared in the distance. Diana could picture the families living in those villas, gathering together in the large rooms and terraces, eating together under pergolas adorned with vines, or groups getting together and having parties on the terraces, calling out to passing boats, making sure they were seen, envied even. Diana would have liked a drink to sip whilst relaxing in the warm sunshine and regretted not bringing one down with them, but there was no way she was attempting those stairs again so soon.

They watched Suzanne and Felipe go down the steps into the sea and swim out into the choppy water. She hoped they would be okay, no more accidents; it was not exactly a haven of health and safety there, which was refreshing, but also a tad worrying when you were in the middle of nowhere. Anna had not even attempted to come down.

The sound of horns honking made her look up to the coast road. She had seen this road so many times in TV and films, but was unprepared for it. The narrow, winding roads were precarious and she had seen cars and scooters drive too fast and take chances. Gianluca was anxious that everyone take care on these roads, should they want to go for a walk. He said someone had been killed only last week, a woman on a scooter, someone she thought Rocco may have known, judging by his expression.

Francesca joined Fleur and Diana on the terrace and settled down with her earphones. She was hoping for a tan by the end of the week. She missed her dog, a Labrador, and thought she would facetime her later.

Anna retired to her room. It was a shame, she would have liked to have joined the girls by the pool, but those stairs were too much for her and she did not want to end up like David. No, she would check in on Facebook and read a little. She was looking forward to dinner tonight, she hoped there would be limoncello to finish the evening.

David cursed himself for being so stupid. Why had he decided to go for a swim in the sea? He had headed down the steps to the sea, the rope 'bannister' not helping much. When he had got to the bottom, Suzanne and Felipe were arriving and he had offered to help, but had slipped and fallen heavily. He had felt the sharp, searing pain in his shoulder immediately, but had been more worried by the fact that he had exposed himself whilst falling; who told him speedos were a good idea at his age? He hoped that Suzanne and Felipe had not noticed. He had wrapped the beach towel around his waist, using one hand, and the pain had been excruciating. They had been very kind and helped him back up the steps to the terrace, where Gianluca had busied himself getting painkillers and a sling to support his arm. David resigned himself to the fact that he would do little cooking this week, but he decided to stay. The villa and surrounding area was so beautiful and the company good and anyway, he was in no rush to go home just yet.

Chris was sitting in bed watching TV on the other side of the world. He looked at the first of the photos he had expected he would receive when she had messaged to say she was off to Italy. The scenery looked stunning and he definitely wished he was there. This woman travelled a lot, she seemed to enjoy life and he was wanting more and more to enjoy it with her. He felt he needed to know once and for all whether this woman was his destiny or not.

The sun was setting and Diana joined Fleur on her balcony before dinner; thinking she must ask Gianluca for a couple of chairs for the balcony. The day had gone by far too quickly and easily and they were both looking forward to dinner and company tonight. They made their way up to the terrace and joined the others. The sun was going down quickly and the lights in the villas and houses on the cliff side were twinkling and casting a magical glow over the sea. It was perfect, peaceful and even better than Diana ever thought it would be.

They sat down to bowls of fennel and orange salad, fresh bread and oils, olives, garlic chicken, aubergine parmigiana—melanzane alla parmigiana, Rocco explained—and tomatoes. The conversation flowed, with everyone talking a little more about themselves and their lives back home, their travels so far, the food they enjoyed to eat and cook and the wine they liked to drink, prompting Gianluca to get another bottle of red from his ever decreasing, not so secret, stash in the kitchen.

At the end of the meal, Gianluca presented a tray with a large bottle of limoncello and small sherry type glasses to the group. He explained that the limoncello was made locally and was an acquired taste and he would not be offended at all if the group did not like it. Diana had been waiting for an opportunity to taste this liqueur, renown in this region. Each had a glass and sipped the sweet lemon liquid. Diana tasted the sweet, intense lemony flavour and she knew she was hooked. She caught a glimpse of the resigned look on Gianluca's face; his budget was definitely going to be tested this week.

Diana took two glasses of Limoncello and joined Fleur on her balcony for a nightcap. Gianluca had arranged for two chairs to be placed on the balcony—Diana briefly wondered who by—and they sat there in the warm evening air, sipping limoncello and looking out to sea. Diana was wondering if Fleur would tell the group why she was leaving early and Fleur was thinking of a way to tell the group she had cancer and was leaving to have surgery on Thursday. She did not want to depress everyone or bring the mood down, but the latter would be inevitable. She had already tipped Gianluca to make sure that Diana would have her room when she left; she had a feeling Felipe was thinking to do the same.

Diana made her way back to her room (cave); she heard Gianluca and Rocco talking at the other end of the corridor. Gianluca was asking Rocco about a woman on a scooter and Rocco was saying, "Mamma mia, Mamma mia." He thought it was her, but it wasn't. She heard the door close and she carried on to her room. In bed, she turned off the light and thought she just couldn't wait for tomorrow, another bucket list moment with a trip to Capri. She and Fleur were going to buy headscarves at the small Amalfi port where they would board the ferry and pretend to be '60s' film stars for the day.

Chapter Five – Monday: Capri

The day dawned; it was obviously sunny, but Diana's room was in gloomy darkness. She could hear people up and about, sounds from the sea below, birds flying over. The room was typical of an Italian villa, but she would be glad to move into Fleur's room tomorrow. It was bright and airy, had balcony doors and wasn't a bit cave like. The only problem was the door, which didn't lock, but she would deal with that tomorrow. Fleur was not bothered by it, even when she was in the shower.

Diana was looking forward to Capri. When she had booked the week cooking in Amalfi, she had not realised this was part of the itinerary, she had just been excited to finally book an Italian cooking holiday, not appreciating there would be day trips too. She had also told Fleur it was in Tuscany and it wasn't until the flights were to be confirmed they realised it was in Amalfi and not Tuscany at all. Just as well the company had booked the flights on their behalf and they had not chosen the option to book themselves, as god knows where they would have ended up. Breakfast was the usual continental affair and she helped David butter his toast, pour his juice and pour his coffee. Then it was off to the minibus with Giovanni to drive into Amalfi, to catch the ferry to Capri. Diana was not looking forward to the ferry; she had been known to feel seasick on a pedalo and even a rowboat on the Hollow Ponds.

The ride to Amalfi along the narrow, winding coast road took a bit longer than she and Giovanni expected. The traffic was heavy, with scooters weaving in and out of the cars and coaches, some pillion passengers taking selfies, the scooters aiming to get where they were going, just that bit quicker. Diana briefly wondered if this was the reason for the death Gianluca had mentioned; was that rider trying to get somewhere just that bit quicker?

The port was small and Fleur and Diana wandered around the few shops, near the marina, looking for scarves. They were going to wear these on the ferry and pretend to be Audrey Hepburn in a 1960s movie, black sunglasses too. Scarves purchased, they met the group in the queue for the ferry. The ferry was busy and they made their way to the outside deck in the hope this would stave off any seasickness. The scarves and glasses turned out to be a very good idea as the crossing to Capri was blustery on the deck as they made their way to the first stop at Positano. Fleur and Diana enjoyed the sea views and sat contentedly watching a succession of day trippers make their way to the front of the boat to take pictures, which was both funny and worrying, particularly the older lady who was hanging on the ropes precariously, just to take that photo of islands that looked like a person laying down. They were glad they sat at the rear, backs to the wall; people sitting at the sides were in the soak zone, splashed all the way.

Diana was very thankful that she had managed to get to Capri without being seasick; kids' travel sickness pills really did work. Disembarking the ferry at Marina Grande, the group made their way to the funicular ticket office, where Gianluca purchased the group's tickets. Diana waved to Rocco, who was talking to a very glamourous woman she didn't recognise. He did not wave back. Instead he hurried off up the narrow streets, full of tourists, and disappeared.

After a brief stroll around the marina area, dotted with yachts of all shapes, sizes and value, they all made their way to the funicular, which climbed slowly and sedately uphill through lemon groves from the Marina Grande to the Piazza Umberto, in the centre of Capri. Diana had a sudden flashback to weekends with her mum to Hastings, and her first funiculars. How exciting it had been, albeit without the views. Diana thought she must have been mistaken about Rocco; he did not meet them at the funicular. Perhaps it was someone else who looked like him, after all, he would not come all this way to source ingredients for dinner tonight.

The view from the piazza was stunning: vivid blue skies, meeting an aquamarine Tyrrhenian Sea, not a cloud in the sky, and intense pinks and greens of the lemon groves only adding to the holiday brochure picture. A cruise liner sat out to sea after bringing in the day trippers, waiting patiently for their return. The group went their own way, arranging to meet for lunch later. Diana enjoyed wandering in and out of the side streets full of tourist shops, laden with lemon soaps, oils, herbs, glasses and decorative plates, stopping to purchase a Caprese salad plate and glasses adorned with lemons, for limoncello when she got home, she thought.

Diana and Fleur walked past the designer boutiques, instead preferring the local food and speciality shops, dodging open air taxis and scooters, and bumped into Anna and Francesca in the Piazza Umberto, joining them for a gin and tonic. They sat and talked easily, like old friends, watching the other tourists and listening to the couple on the next table complaining about everything, and questioned how they could be so negative in such a beautiful, bustling, lively place. They left the café and the moaning couple and made their way to meet the group and walk together to a local restaurant in time for lunch. The small narrow streets led to beautiful views once again, but this time with Vesuvius residing proudly over the whole scene, cloud topped, dark and brooding as usual.

Suzanne and Felipe had quickly left the group when the funicular arrived; Suzanne had mapped a walking route on the iPad which would be enough steps and exercise for the day, especially as they missed their morning swim in the ocean this morning as they had to catch the minibus. She was enjoying the holiday and they were both getting on well with the group, although she could have done without the drama of David. Felipe exhaled deeply. He would have preferred to sit in a piazza sipping a cold beer with the others for at least some of the morning, rather than walk ten thousand steps, or whatever the target was this morning.

David stood with the group when they got off the funicular, admiring the views. This was when things felt a little difficult for him; he knew he would be on his own for a few hours. The group had already paired off, Fleur and Diana, Francesca and Anna, Suzanne and Felipe. He did not want to impose; perhaps he should have asked Barbara after all.

Anna was quite happy to have a few hours on her own. She would look in the shops for a bit and then find a nice café to sit and watch the world go by, possibly with a gin and tonic or two. Francesca was on mission; she had done her research and knew there were a few designer shops here and where they were. She intended to look for something to wear to an event later this month, something that she could not get at home, a dress maybe.

The group settled down to lunch. The restaurant owner insisted on providing the Italian names for all the dishes and listing the ingredients: insalata caprese, a salad of mozzarella, tomatoes, green basil, salt and olive oil; ensalada de pulpo, octopus, mixed with lemon juice, salt, pepper, oregano and garlic; scialatielli, pasta with courgette; pezzogna, sea bream. Desert was torta caprese, chocolate and almond cake, served with a small, icy glass of limoncello. The table was also laden with olives and fresh bread, with bottles of olive oil and the tastiest balsamic vinegar.

Over lunch Diana, Gianluca and Fleur talked about bucket lists. Diana wanted to travel to Cinque Terre and Portofino, hopefully with Fleur. Gianluca wanted to return to Sicily and settle down. Gianluca regaled his travels to the group, but lamented he had no savings to settle down and buy a house. Fleur suggested buying a lottery ticket and an idea was born. Fleur, Diana and Gianluca would club together and purchase several tickets today, agreeing to share the proceeds should they win. Diana would travel, Gianluca would buy a luxury yacht and Fleur wasn't sure what she wanted to do with hers; she would think about it later.

Everyone agreed that lunch was a huge success as they made their way back to the funicular for the journey back to Marina Grande. At the bottom, Gianluca, Fleur and Diana slipped away to purchase lottery tickets before the ferry ride home. They agreed to scratch them off over dinner that night.

The ferry ride back to Amalfi was uneventful and luckily, Diana was not sick, despite the lunch. She had been particularly worried after having the octopus. The group had an hour in Amalfi before returning to the villa and split up to explore the small town. Looking up to the cliffs and Amalfi coast road above, Diana briefly imagined driving through the tortuously winding tunnel cut into the cliff above with the arched glassless windows, giving peeks of the magnificent sea view as you drove through it; She imagined someone driving dangerously at high speed, chased by a villain, knowing a mistake could send him careering over the edge of cliffs to a sheer drop.

Leaving the marina, they found the whole area very picturesque, with lots of narrow streets, abundant with shops and cafes, leading to a square looking up to a huge cathedral. Looking in her trusty travel guide, a different article for every trip, Diana informed Fleur this was the Cattedrale di Sant'Andrea; a medieval cathedral housing the relics of the apostle, Saint Andrew, just in case she wanted to go inside. A couple were having photographs taken on the steps leading to the cathedral, having just got married, and everyone cheered in the cafés below, celebrating their union and genuine happiness.

Fleur and Diana revelled in the shops selling flavoured oils, pastas and herbs, and one which had a display of baskets overflowing with the biggest lemons they had ever seen. This prompted the posting of a photo, resulting in some very funny comments about big lemons.

The group came together again in the Piazza Del Duomo and enjoyed a drink before the ride back to the villa. While the others were talking, Diana nipped off to find a local bookshop with Anna to see if she could purchase Rocco's cookbook (she wanted him to sign it), but the shopkeeper did not understand what she was asking for, even when she showed her a picture of the book on her mobile. Strangely, though, she felt the woman in the queue behind her did.

Back at the villa, Fleur was feeling apprehensive. She had enjoyed a few days without thinking about what was coming, now she could not put it out of her mind, she was leaving tomorrow, Tuesday; Wednesday was preparing for surgery on Thursday. She was not looking forward to explaining to the group why she was leaving early, it made it all too real.

Diana watched Fleur go back to her room; she knew she was anxious and why. She was not looking forward to tomorrow either.

Anna wondered what was wrong. Fleur and Diana were a happy, positive pair, but right now she could tell something was wrong. She wanted to ask if she could help, but did not want to pry.

Francesca relaxed in her room and Facetimed her husband and her dog; she was missing them both. They had been married ten years and were still happy together. Her friends thought this was because they had no children and, therefore, no stress. She had decided to stay the week in the villa and not hot foot it back to Rome, which was her original intention. The group was nice, a mixture of people who were all getting on and enjoying the cooking and the trip. She was looking forward to the next lesson and having time to herself this week; she would definitely look into that application after all.

David was struggling to get dressed. He had managed to have a shower, by sitting in the bath, but zips and belts were difficult one handed; he had no choice but to ask Gianluca. He would make his way to the terrace for dinner, holding up his trousers and hoping he didn't fall and break the other shoulder on the way down.

Rocco was busy preparing an evening meal of salad, mixed bean salad, herby potatoes and sea bream, bought at the port today, finished with a lemon cake for dessert. He was feeling agitated. He had to produce a meal which appeared to have meant hours in the kitchen; he also felt sure Diana had seen him in Capri today.

The meal was enjoyed with copious amounts of red and white wine from the region. Diana took a photo of the red wine with the intention of looking for it when she got home, and if she could not find it, there was always online.

Fleur explained to the group why she was leaving tomorrow, but with her usual positivity, pointed out she was looking forward to perky boobs after the surgery, without the cost of a boob job, which lightened the mood a little. Diana looked out of the open window to the night view. The pitch black of the night sky, broken with twinkling coloured lights from the restaurants and villas on the cliffs, created a bluey-green sheen in shards over the sea. She would miss this view desperately and took a photo so she could remember it, but it did not do it justice. She was not sure what view was better, day or evening.

As dessert was finished, Gianluca brought out the three lottery tickets purchased in Capri and Diana, Fleur and Gianluca had one each to scratch off. Suzanne and Felipe scoffed at the idea, David took no notice, Francesca looked intrigued and Anna said she wanted to join in if more tickets were purchased. Felipe offered a euro to scratch off the silver coating and Gianluca went first. The anticipation grew, Diana was sure she could feel the others wanting the tickets to win and lose at the same time. Her imagination wandered; she could see herself in a Winnebago travelling across Australia, New Zealand or from Miami to the Keys, or maybe all them. She could, after all, be a millionaire. Gianluca pictured himself on the deck of his yacht with his own bodyguards and Stefania, his beautiful Sicilian wife, sunbathing on the deck. Fleur just wanted to know if they had won anything; she wanted some good news. Felipe now wished he had not scoffed and been asked to chip in. Anna felt excited; she wanted them to win something. The first ticket won fifteen euros, the second ticket won another scratch card and the third card won another twenty euros.

"Well," sighed Diana, "if only we had bought more, who knows what we could have won," and she mentally watched her Winnebago drive off without her and disappear in a puff of exhaust fumes.

They decided to pool the thirty-five euros and spend it all on more lottery scratch cards. Anna wanted to chip in as she would like to visit her son in Australia with her winnings. David was keen too and said he would like to win enough to take a luxury couple's holiday in the Caribbean, something he thought Emma may like. Francesca said she would like to win so she could take a sabbatical, and looked quizzically at David; she thought his partner was Barbara. Rocco was not listening. He was busy on his mobile and Diana felt sure he was avoiding her. Suzanne and Felipe looked at each other and Felipe said well, it would be rude not to join in the fun. Everyone laughed at this and it was agreed, they all chipped in five euros each. Gianluca would get more tickets, one each, tomorrow, which they would scratch off at the end of dinner tomorrow night. Diana, Fleur and Gianluca would buy more tickets with their winnings too. Diana would message Fleur and let her know the outcome.

Chapter Six –Farewell Fleur

Fleur woke up with a start. The sun pouring in through the balcony door had warmed one side of her body. She looked at the view and wished she could have stayed longer. She had only had one cooking lesson; still there was one more trip and cheese tasting to look forward to. She finished packing the last few items in her case and took a deep breath and left the room. She walked towards Diana's room along the corridor and knocked. Diana opened almost immediately, pausing only to grab her mobile before leaving. Fleur knew Diana was looking forward to moving into her room later; she was glad she had suggested it before someone else had put dibs on it. Diana would enjoy it, although she must remember to tell her about the fishermen in the mornings.

Breakfast over, it was time to go to Ravello and on the way, stop at a mozzarella farm. The minibus awaited them at the top of the villa and the group took their seats. Funny how they all sat in the same seat as before, Fleur thought; Suzanne and Felipe at the front with Giovanni; Anna and Francesca in the back and David, Diana and Fleur in the middle row. Diana pondered if the others would get annoyed if she sat somewhere other than the middle row and it reminded her of the time she had gone to an exercise class and put her mat down near the teacher as she was new to Pilates, causing a near riot when she refused to move when one of the long-time attendees said it was her spot on the floor and could she move. Anna felt like a naughty child, banished to the back of the vehicle.

The drive to Ravello, via the mozzarella farm, took them along winding roads, high up into the mountains, with aromatic lemon groves growing in the most unusual places on the side of the cliff. surrounded by colourful flowers and quaint stone walls in the middle of nowhere.

The group joined two 'farmers' in a large clinical looking barn type building, who demonstrated how to make mozzarella. The room had stainless steel troughs and vats of hot water and a milky liquid, some of which had been spilt on the floor and was in puddles, which the group did their best to avoid. Using long wooden paddles and their hands and arms to stretch and pull the cheese, the two men talked to Gianluca who translated and explained what was happening and why. The mozzarella was rolled into balls by hand and dropped into the vats of warm milky liquid to rest, like a floatation tank, Diana thought. When the demonstration was finished, trays of freshly made mozzarella, as well as ricotta, were wheeled in on a trolley with bread for the group to taste. Diana asked why they were sampling ricotta too, as they had only seen mozzarella being made. Gianluca explained how ricotta was produced from the whey left over from the making of buffalo mozzarella, so it made sense for the farm to make both. After a lot of oohing and aahing, all agreed it was the best and freshest cheese they had ever tasted.

The group thanked the farmers and continued their journey to Ravello, the minibus travelling along more winding roads until it stopped in a cobbled street and the group alighted. Following Gianluca through narrow alleyways, they suddenly turned and found themselves in another beautiful square, cafes on three sides, facing the steps to the duomo. The square was edged with baskets and terracotta pots with trailing foliage and pink flowers, and they led you up the steps, steering you to the big brass door of the duomo.

The mountaintop views from the square were impressive and the medieval stone walls and archways gave Diana glimpses of the constricted, winding streets beyond. The group continued to follow Gianluca as they explored the area surrounding the duomo and Diana wondered who lived in the houses, reached only by treacherous looking steep steps from a courtyard or through a tiny wrought iron gate onto a covered terrace, with walls covered in brightly decorated plates of all shapes and sizes; the people living here obviously could not be anyone elderly or if it was, they must be housebound.

Their short walking tour with Gianluca took them on a loop and the group ended back in the square, where they separated and wandered off lazily to look in the local shops. Diana, Fleur and Gianluca took the opportunity to buy lottery tickets for themselves and the group. Suzanne and Felipe went to find the Villa Cimbrone and build up their steps for the day. David sat in the square with a beer and waited for the others to return. Anna went to have a look inside the duomo and lit a candle whilst she was there; Francesca stood looking out over the lemon groves. She had made a decision; she would definitely complete the application tonight.

The journey back to the villa for lunch was quite sombre. Fleur was going home as soon as they got back. Diana looked out of the window at the views; she still could not believe she was here. Gianluca opened the gates to the villa as they approached; he was always anxious not to hold up the traffic on the coast road.

The group helped Fleur get her things from her room and take them to the top. She was travelling to the airport in the same minibus that had taken them to Ravello. Fleur said her goodbyes and wished everyone a happy rest of the week and asked for plenty of photos to be messaged to her, as well as news if they won the lottery of course. Diana would be calling Fleur on

Thursday evening for an update on how the surgery had gone.

Diana waited until everyone had said their goodbyes and best wishes and Fleur was in the minibus about to go. She went towards her, finding it hard to hold back the tears. Fleur looked at Diana. She could see she was about to cry. She wondered again why they had not spent much time together until recently. Fleur looked at Diana, "Don't," she said. "Go, or I'll cry too." Diana stepped back, the sliding door closed and the minibus moved off, edging out onto the Amalfi coast road to make the trip back to Naples.

Diana left the group and hurried down the steps to her room. She sat on the bed and cried. Fleur had been so brave, so positive, but now it had become all so real. She was anxious for her, scared, she could not imagine how Fleur must feel. She also felt guilty; she had wanted to leave with her, but Fleur had been adamant. Diana was to stay the week and they would do the trip again next year.

The cooking lesson today was after lunch, Diana was thankful; it would help to take her mind off things even for a little while. Diana would move rooms after the lesson had finished. She had not really unpacked, so it would be easy to do. She felt she should move quickly, or she may lose the room with a view, and a balcony, to Suzanne and Felipe.

Chapter Seven – Second Cooking Lesson

The group assembled at the large wooden table on the terrace, aprons on and iPhones and iPads at the ready. Wooden pasta boards had been laid out again, together with a recipe sheet and knife on each. The large brightly patterned bowls which Diana now knew were specific to the Amalfi Coast and very expensive, were used to hold the ingredients for today's lesson.

The bowls were lined up along the centre of the table again, each filled with sage, breadcrumbs, parmesan, eggs and walnuts. Rocco appeared from the small narrow doorway of the kitchen with ricotta, purchased by Gianluca that morning, explaining this would be used for the ravioli that day, which would be filled with ricotta and walnuts and drizzled with a sage butter dressing.

Second Cooking Lesson

Ravioli

00 flour
eggs
Salt and pepper
Extra virgin Olive Oil
tepid water
buffalo ricotta (purchased at Mozzarella farm by Gianluca)
walnuts – finely chopped
breadcrumbs
parmesan
pinch of nutmeg

Like the first lesson, Rocco allocated jobs: Diana to finely chop the walnuts, "But not too fine, we don't want breadcrumbs," Rocco said, sounding exasperated; Felipe and Suzanne to measure five hundred grammes of ricotta per person; Francesca to measure one hundred grammes of Parmesan and breadcrumbs per person; Anna to give two large eggs everyone; and David gave out the mixing bowls with his one good arm.

David watched as everyone mixed their filling together for the ravioli and had a quick mix with Rocco, whilst he held the bowl. Two cups of pasta flour was poured onto each board, with instructions to form a crater in the middle, "To resemble Vesuvius," joked Rocco. Five eggs were then cracked into the crater, with a splash of oil, salt and pepper, and a few drops of the warm water. After gently whisking the eggy mixture together, the group watched as Rocco tenderly and lovingly worked the ingredients into a sticky mixture, then a dough, by pulling the yellowy dusty flour into the eggy mixture from around the sides in a slow and methodical manner.

Once the group had all reached this stage too, Rocco flamboyantly flung more 00 flour onto the boards from a height—*a bit dramatic*, thought Diana—and began kneading the dough, stressing the importance of lovingly, but firmly caressing and kneading the soft mound with the heel of your hand, pressing forward and turning, forward and turning until the dough was smooth and when pressed with a finger, the indent bouncing back. The group busied themselves making their pasta, laughing at themselves as they kneaded 'Rocco style'. The soft mounds were then covered with cling film and left to rest and the group enjoyed a glass of prosecco, which Gianluca had ready on the side.

Anna sat at the top of the table watching Diana. She could tell she was enjoying the lesson, but that she was also anxious, she seemed to stop laughing sometimes as if she remembered, she should not be enjoying herself. Anna hoped she would enjoy the rest of the week and not worry too much about Fleur. Suzanne was also looking at Diana posting a photo for her friends and family to see; she hoped she would not have to look after her for the rest of the week.

David was enjoying helping Rocco, who he felt was kind enough to try to include him. His arm still strapped up to prevent moving his shoulder, meant there was little he could do. One thing he had discovered was he liked prosecco, definitely something he would introduce to Barbara when he got home. Felipe wanted a beer and made a mental note to give Gianluca some money to pick up a few beers next time he went shopping. Francesca felt restless; she wanted to get back to her room and apply before she chickened out and changed her mind, again.

Gianluca asked when they were going to check their lottery tickets and they all agreed they would do it later, over dinner tonight. He felt lucky today; he looked out to sea and was almost sure he saw his yacht sailing by with Stefania waving to him from the deck.

The group assembled around the table once more and rolled out their dough until thin enough and it almost covered the board; the thin, yellowy sheets were cut into five centimetre wide strips. A spoon of ricotta and walnut filling was placed in the centre along the length of strip, with space between each filling for two fingers. Another strip was placed on top and pressed gently together in the spaces and edges. The ravioli was finished by cutting into squares and crimping the edges with a fork.

Gradually each board became abundant with freshly made ravioli, some strewn across the board, like Anna's, others like Diana's in neat lines. Diana looked at her orderly ravioli; she was always organised, it even showed in her ravioli. A former colleague had often said she should think outside the box, but given they had been the most disorganised person she had ever had the misfortune to work with, with an office that resembled an episode of *Hoarders from Hell*, she wasn't about to take advice from them.

Rocco called the group to the small kitchen where a pan of boiling water was bubbling away and a small pan with melted butter was sizzling on a low heat on the stove top. One portion of ravioli was dropped into the water whilst torn sage leaves were added to the butter. After three minutes the ravioli was fished out of the boiling water, gently shaken to remove any excess and then tossed in the sizzling butter only briefly, before being poured into a pink and white bowl, decorated with what Diana thought looked like white pigs. The local plates, Diana had found, were lovely, expensive and sometimes curiously decorated; she would give the pig plates a miss. Everyone picked up a fork and took a portion of ravioli to try, each exclaiming how delicious it was and how they were sure that must be their pasta they were eating.

The lesson ended with more prosecco on the terrace, Rocco would be cooking the rest of the ravioli for dinner tonight.

The group had free time until dinner in a few hours' time. Diana went to her room and began to move her clothes and toiletries into Fleur's room; it didn't take very long. She stood on the balcony looking out to sea, watching the boats and ferries come and go and watching people in the villas nearby. She could hear raised voices nearby, heated, a woman's voice accusing someone of cheating. Diana looked along the balcony and then went to the bedroom door and opened it, looking along the corridor to the large conservatory room at the opposite end to her old room. She could see shadows of people moving about through the glass in the door and wondered who it could be. As far as she knew, there was only the group and hosts here, yet she could definitely hear a woman's voice that she did not recognise. Maybe it was from the next villa; she could hear children laughing too.

Suzanne and Felipe decided to spend a couple of hours at the pool. Suzanne took her iPad and busied herself organising the photos she had taken so far and sending a few off to friends and family. She wanted them to know how beautiful it was in Amalfi, plus pose just that little bit. She was also going to search local suppliers of ceramic patio tables and chairs, which she thought would look ideal on the patio at home, next to the recently built brick pizza oven. Felipe watched Suzanne messaging photos and wondered only briefly who to, as he was more interested in how he was going to avoid paying thousands for a ceramic table and chairs. He wondered where Diana and Francesca were, they were fun to be around.

David retired to the terrace by the kitchen with his book and a bottle of prosecco. Looking out to sea, he wished he had company to admire the view with and wondered where everyone had gone. He thought about joining Suzanne and Felipe, but decided against risking the stairs down to the pool again. He thought about knocking on Francesca's door to see if she wanted to join him on the terrace, but thought better of it; she had seemed rather preoccupied. Anna seemed a little annoyed at him as he had referred to her as the Miss Marple of the group earlier and Diana, well best leave her to get over Fleur leaving. What a brave woman Fleur was, put his shoulder problem into perspective. It wasn't until sometime after wishing he had company that he suddenly worried that he had not thought of Barbara first.

Anna lay on the bed in her room with the intention of having a nap, but David's comment about her being the Miss Marple of the group had irritated her. After all, she had only asked who Emma was and was she related to Barbara? Granted she may be the more mature one of the group, but she didn't think of herself as a bespectacled elderly spinster quite yet. Was this how people viewed her? Anna got up and looked in the mirror at her silver hair and what her husband had often described as mischievous blue eyes. She didn't think she dressed like an elderly woman, favouring flowing Indian inspired tops and linen trousers. Anna heard raised voices and went to the door and looked out, in time to hear something smash and Diana's door close. She thought the voice belonged to Rocco, but did not recognise the woman's voice, something for Miss Marple to investigate after all she thought, after her nap.

Francesca sat at her laptop looking at the government website. She stared at the blinking cursor which indicated her application for a birth relative to apply for entry in the Adoption Contact Register was nearly complete. Just one more click. She felt sick, how would she explain this to Mark? She clicked confirm and paid, it was done; now she would have to wait and see if anyone was looking for her. She could not bring herself to think that there could be a wish for no contact registered; that her daughter did not want to meet her.

Gianluca looked at the lottery tickets and thought one of these could make him rich tonight. For a brief minute he contemplated slipping one of them in his pocket. He looked out of the window and pictured his yacht one more time; a yacht that not even one winning ticket would buy, but still he could dream and a big win could still change his life forever. He looked at the tickets in his hand, sighed and put them all together in his back pocket. He could not cheat the others, he would not feel right. Tonight they would scratch off the numbers and win together.

Rocco sat on the couch in the conservatory and looked at his chefs' whites hanging on the clothes horse drying. He was sure that others must have heard her. He had tried to let her down gently, explaining he was sorry, it was not her, it was him, he wanted to be a good father and stay with his partner, but she would not give up, he was beginning to think she would never leave him alone.

Rocco thought back, he had met her on a previous cooking holiday a year ago after which she had appeared randomly whenever he was away from his family. He thought she had followed him and his whereabouts through social media, so he had stopped posting as much, but knew she was somehow 'following' his friends. He hoped he would work things out before he returned home to Sicily in the summer; his partner and the family would not be happy to say the least. He had not discussed this with Gianluca, although he thought Gianluca suspected something and was judging him. Gianluca had asked him if there was anything wrong on the night of the fatal scooter accident and he had felt bad, for a split second he had wanted it to be her on the scooter, then his problems would be over.

The group assembled on the terrace for pre-dinner drinks and took it in turns to peek through the open windows to the small dining room. The bowls and plates of salad, breads, cold meats, bruschetta and olives looked delicious, as did the bottles of red wine. This would be followed by the ravioli prepared earlier, and Diana and Anna hoped for limoncello later.

The group sat down and each took turns to help David with drinks and food from the table. Conversation flowed easily, with snippets of information about family life dropped in casually, as if they had known each other much longer than just a few days. The warm breeze wafted in through the small open windows, bringing in the faint sounds from the sea below, the cliffs above and other villas nearby. The glimmering lights of villas and small villages built on the cliff edges from the sea upwards again cast a magical yellowy green light out over the sea and Diana inhaled deeply. She wanted to remember this view when she got home, and the calm feelings the view produced. She had a feeling her album would contain photos of food, drink and night time views, interspersed with an odd photo of herself and others.

Gianluca cleared away the dishes and brought in a tray containing a bottle of limoncello and the delicate sherry style glasses. On the tray was a pile of lottery tickets. Each would scratch off a card tonight. *How fantastic would it be to win*, he thought and then worried if it would bring happiness. Rocco looked at the tray and the tickets; how silly he thought, then worried they might actually win and he would be the one who would be forever known as 'the one who missed out'.

The limoncello was poured out and the tickets distributed. They each decided to take a turn and scratch off the grey substance covering the symbols and numbers that could decide a different future. Everyone listened to Gianluca as he explained carefully what to do to ensure the ticket would be valid if they won.

Anna went first, laughing and lamenting that she never won anything, which unfortunately continued to be the case. Francesca took the euro and briefly thought how many dogs she could have with a big win, maybe even a kennels. She scratched off the panel to reveal a win of another scratch card. David was next and Francesca held the ticket, whilst he scratched away, blowing the little grey discarded bits across the dining table. His ticket won ten euros. Diana was next, her stomach churned as she desperately wanted that trip in the Winnebago, but a share of ten euros wouldn't do that. Gianluca looked out the window and saw his yacht moored, lights on and music playing, the deck staged with champagne on ice and dimmed lighting. His card produced fifteen euros and his yacht sailed away into the distance, disappearing into the horizon as he pictured the empty bottle of champagne tossed overboard with a splash.

Suzanne and Felipe were next and Felipe passed the card to Suzanne, who scratched the panels quickly and was surprised at herself for being excited at the possibility of winning; it was another scratch card. Everyone sat back whilst Gianluca collected the winning cards: two more scratch cards and thirty-five euros. More limoncello was consumed and Anna suggested they pool their winnings and buy more lottery tickets tomorrow. Felipe said it would be rude not to and everyone laughed. It was agreed, Gianluca would redeem their winnings and buy more scratch cards tomorrow and they would do the same again after dinner tomorrow. They toasted their imaginary winnings over more limoncello and then went their separate ways to bed.

Diana made her way to her new room; she changed and opened the balcony doors. She lay in bed looking out at the blackness of the sea, which was both calming and a bit frightening at the same time. The night sky was full of twinkling stars, so many of them brightly shining, causing more reflections on the bobbing sea. She thought of Fleur and hoped she was not alone. She fell asleep to the sounds of the sea, thinking at home she would normally have all the doors and windows very securely locked.

Chapter Eight – Wednesday

Diana awoke to the sun streaming through the balcony doors and the sounds of birds flying by. She could hear the splashing of a boat and voices, although she could not work out what they were saying or how near they were. She looked at the time and lazily made her way to the bathroom, completely tiled like her old room in the villa, in bright, orange and blue busy patterned tiles, but it was open and airy and no wall of exposed cliff. The window had no blind, but she was not worried, she was overlooking the sea after all. She opened the window— Fleur had said the room got steamy—and started the shower. The water was hot and she enjoyed the freedom of a large walk-in shower with a view to remember; she felt like she was showering outside. As she towelled herself dry, she could hear the voices again, this time laughing and excitable, calling 'signora, signora'. Diana looked up to see a small fishing boat with a group of fishermen waving at her; she ducked down and heard laughter. *Bloody hell!* she thought Fleur could have warned her about that rather than the bathroom got steamy.

Francesca anxiously tapped at her laptop; she knew it expecting far too much to think there would be any reply or contact today. She waited for David to head down for breakfast. She knew he needed help with dressing, but she did not want to button his shirt or worse, zip his shorts. She would leave this to Gianluca.

David made his way down the steps to the breakfast area, hoping Gianluca would be there alone. He did not like relying on him to help him finish dressing, but he had little choice. He had managed to have a shower of sorts, but it had taken him twice as long as usual and he had been petrified he would slip and break the other arm. He wondered if Barbara would help him when he got home.

Suzanne and Felipe were making their way up the stairs for breakfast. Suzanne was going to ask Gianluca to stop at a ceramic factory on the way to Positano tomorrow; she had researched on her iPad and the ceramics factory was literally on the way, not far from the villa. She had her eye on a table and four chairs, wrought iron base with ceramic hand painted designs of flowers and lemons in vivid blues and yellows. They were quite costly, running to a good few thousand euros, but it would be an investment. Felipe was wondering if he could quietly slip Gianluca a few euros to avoid the factory.

Anna sat in a chair looking out to sea, her book in her lap. She had been up for some time and could hear some of the others getting up, getting ready for breakfast. She had watched Suzanne and Felipe go down the cliff steps to the sea and take their morning swim. She wondered if they knew the villas in the area emptied their sewage into the sea.

Gianluca was busy preparing breakfast for the group and prepping for Rocco and the next cookery lesson this morning. He was looking forward to the trip to Positano tomorrow; there was a lovely bar on the seafront he particularly liked and thought the group would enjoy, although he was not sure the waitress would want to see him again, she had not been impressed when he had asked her to share the cost of a meal on a recent date. She had left, not staying for dessert, and he had not followed, the Neapolitan baba had been too good to leave. He had regaled this story to the group last night and could not really understand why they had laughed and exclaimed, "Oh Luca, what are you like." He heard David approaching and knew he would need help with his zips and buttons; he put down the coffee pot and went to help.

Rocco was also preparing the ingredients for their next lesson, a simple fish dish, gnocchi and struffoli recipes today. He had not heard anything further from her, he hoped she had got the message, gone home and would leave him alone now.

Gianluca had prepared breakfast which included Sicilian favourites of coffee granita and slices of brioche to eat with ice cream. Diana decided on the brioche and ice cream, as she liked to try dishes she had not had before and besides, she noticed the lemon marmalade had not made an appearance today. They all enjoyed the granita, even though it was very strong.

Once breakfast was finished, the group assembled on the terrace, awaiting the sign from Rocco and Gianluca that the lesson was ready to begin. They offered to help, but were told firmly to finish their teas and coffees. They watched them take bowls of ingredients to the large wooden table on the terrace, already laden with the pasta boards, knives and recipe sheets. The group put on their red aprons and joined the pair on the terrace.

Third Cooking Lesson

Gnocchi, Fish and Struffoli

Gnocchi

1 kilogram of potatoes
1 egg
400g plain flour
Salt

Rocco explained that he had boiled the potatoes in their skins for about forty-five minutes and then left them to cool. Once cooled, he had peeled the potatoes and put them through a potato ricer, one he had bought in Capri at quite a cost to his budget, he thought and something he would not be leaving at the villa.

As with previous lessons, Rocco assigned tasks to the group until everyone, except David, had a pasta board with a mound of potatoes, flour and an egg. Each followed Rocco, by making a crater with the potato adding flour and egg to the middle. Pinches of salt were added and the ingredients carefully mixed together until the mixture became dough that was slightly sticky and all the flour was incorporated. Rocco explained the importance of folding and pressing, not kneading, until the dough was firm and pliable. When everyone reached this point, a dusting of flour was sprinkled over the doughs and the group rested. David had busied himself helping to fold and press with Rocco, using his one good hand.

Rocco became excited as it was now time for the tricky bit, he explained, as he demonstrated how to make the small, perfectly formed gnocchi shapes. He began by rolling the dough into long thin sausages and then cutting inch long shapes, making sure they were very lightly floured at all times. He picked up the small shapes and very lightly, rolled them along the back of a fork, gently flicking them away from the fork at the very end. This method left an imprint of the ridges of the fork on the small shape, which Rocco said were vital as it helped the gnocchi to hold the sauce.

The group began rolling and cutting and soon there were howls of laughter as they tried to repeat the process of rolling the dough shapes along a fork. After about half an hour, the pasta boards, and the table, had a light dusting of flour and were littered with a variety of doughy shapes of all sizes, resembling small white creatures nesting on the boards. Diana had enjoyed this lesson; she loved gnocchi and looked at her floury board of plump little mounds with pride, taking a photo to post later.

Rocco explained he would cook the gnocchi in boiling salted water and serve with melted garlic butter and Parmesan shavings. This would accompany the fish they were going to prepare next.

While the group enjoyed a glass of prosecco, Rocco and Gianluca took the gnocchi to the kitchen for cooking later, cleared the table a little and then returned with a large platter of fish, one for everyone, and a tray of small bowls with various ingredients. Rocco explained this would be a simple dish as everyone was going to prepare the fish for him to cook later with the gnocchi. Diana sighed with relief that the fish had been prepared; she had thought for one awful moment she was going to have to gut a fish, or whatever they called it. Luckily this had been done and all she had to do was stuff the cavity with smashed garlic cloves, lemon, salt, pepper and thyme. The prepared fish were placed on a platter, drizzled with olive oil and taken to the kitchen;

the group meanwhile was sent to wash their hands like naughty children.

Next was struffoli, which Diana learned were small deep fried honey balls traditionally served at Christmas time in Italy.

Struffoli

Eggs
Sugar
Soft butter
00 flour
Zest of an orange and a lemon
Baking powder
Salt
Honey
Limoncello
Edible sprinkles
Sunflower oil to cook

Everyone regrouped at the large table which Gianluca had cleared and prepared with clean pasta boards and bowls of ingredients in the middle. More craters were made with the flour and sugar, filling the middle with eggs, butter, baking powder, salt and zest. Once again, the group worked the ingredients into dough and then let it rest.

Once rested, both the dough and the group, it was time to shape the dough into small balls, the size of a small cherry tomato, by rolling them between the palms. David was able to pinch off small pieces and roll them into balls on a floured pasta board and he enjoyed being part of the lesson, soon having a pile of balls which he found hard to contain with one hand as they kept rolling off the board. Gianluca came to his rescue and placed all the ones he made on a tray, rescuing them from their fate as they rolled towards the edge of the table. At the end of the session there was a mountain of small fluffy balls which Rocco and Gianluca collected and took to the kitchen.

The morning was drawing to a close, but before the lesson ended, they were going to watch Rocco deep fry and finish off a helping of the struffoli balls and cook one fish to serve for tasting with a portion of gnocchi.

The group gathered in the kitchen where there were a lot of pans on the hob: a pan of oil heating for the struffoli; two smaller shallow pans, one with warmed honey, one with only a small amount of oil; one with boiling water. Diana disliked cooking with hot oil as it scared her since a fire at her gran's house when she was small. Rocco took one fish and gently laid it in the pan with olive oil, some of which he spooned over the fish. One portion of gnocchi was softly dropped into a pan of boiling water and Suzanne was asked to remove them as soon as they floated to the top. The fish was turned and basted again with the oil, both dishes taking only minutes to cook. The fish was served on a platter and the gnocchi tossed in melted garlic butter and topped with Parmesan shavings. "Mamma mia," cried Rocco, "taste, taste," he encouraged, passing around forks. He was anxious for his kitchen to be clear as soon as possible.

Rocco gently dropped a handful of struffoli balls in the hot oil which sizzled fiercely as they met each other. He added a glass of limoncello to the warm honey, stirring it through. Anna thought, *what a waste of limoncello*, as she was not really a dessert person. The small balls cooked very quickly and Rocco fished the lightly browned balls out of the oil and dropped them in the honey, swirling them around and then gently removing them, honey dripping off in delicate spools of sticky liquid. He dropped the honeyed balls onto a plate and then ostentatiously threw sprinkles over them from a great height shouting, "Finito!" Diana caught Gianluca rolling his eyes, quietly thanking Rocco for the job of clearing up the sprinkles which were now scattered over many surfaces around the kitchen. The result was a delicious looking plate of sticky golden balls, like a plate of miniature doughnuts Diana thought, which were quickly devoured. Anna thought maybe she could be a dessert person after all.

The group declared the morning's lesson another huge success and looked forward to lunch in a short time. The lesson ended and Rocco shooed everyone out of the kitchen so he could prepare the lunch; he was anxious to be on time, he had things to do this afternoon.

The group settled on the terrace and Gianluca brought a tray with prosecco and glasses, a welcome glass of chilled, bubbling liquid that Felipe found surprisingly refreshing after the hot kitchen. Gianluca left them to help themselves and returned to the kitchen to help Rocco with lunch. The group had a free afternoon and he was going shopping and to buy more lottery tickets. He wondered what Rocco was up to.

Lunch was relaxed, enjoyed with local red and white wine. Rocco had put together big bowls of salads to accompany the fish and gnocchi and the group were eager to taste the labours of the morning's cooking lesson. The golden honey balls were served with soft creamy gelato and Gianluca finished the meal with a tray of very strong coffee, which Diana tried, but again failed, to finish. Gianluca excused himself and said he was off shopping, which would include claiming the two scratch cards won last night and winnings to spend on new scratch cards, including miliardario scratch cards which cost more than the average lottery ticket but the winnings were higher. The group would scratch off the little grey pictures of wads of money tonight after dinner.

Rocco declined their offer to join in and wandered off to the kitchen to tidy up and prepare for the evening meal. She had texted him earlier and he had given in; he was meeting her in Amalfi this afternoon to tell her once and for all, it was over. He thought it would be something better to do face to face. Diana watched Rocco leave and head to the kitchen, he seemed quiet and lost in thought. She knew he was going into Amalfi and wondered if he would let her tag along, save a cab fare, which were really expensive. His mutterings from the kitchen made her stay silent. He obviously had something he needed to do, but not necessarily wanted to do. She would change and spend the afternoon in the sun, the upper terraces had loungers and she could sort her photos and listen to music.

Suzanne and Felipe had decided to go for a walk along the coast road, despite Gianluca's attempts to deter them with horror stories of fatal accidents and fast cars. They promised to be careful and set off. Felipe knew Suzanne wanted to reach the ten thousand steps per day average, but more importantly, make her way to the ceramics factory that was somewhere nearby. He wanted to find somewhere that served beer, as nice as prosecco was.

Anna retired to her room for a shower and a nap. She watched Rocco go into the conservatory area at the end of the corridor and shut the door. He seemed troubled and Anna was sure there must be a woman involved somewhere. Perhaps he was seeing someone, perhaps she was here the other day when she heard voices. Perhaps she would not take no for an answer.

Anna thought it a mystery why some women chased men who obviously were not available, but then maybe he had been and now he wasn't. Her mind wandered; perhaps he could not shake a former lover, a holiday liaison. Well, perhaps he should be faithful then and be thankful for his partner and son he talked about. Anna stopped and chided herself; she did not know the full picture so who was she to judge. Perhaps there was something to David's Miss Marple reference after all.

Francesca changed in her room with the plan to join Diana on the terrace. She gathered her bag and sun cream and stopped briefly to check her emails on her laptop and there it was. The unmistakable unread email, the one she had hoped for and feared at the same time; an email about her entry in the Adoption Contact Register, an email that could say there is a wish for no contact registered. An email she had not expected to receive so quickly, if at all.

Suddenly the years vanished and she was sitting in the hospital room alone, holding a small baby, a baby conceived on a travelling holiday to Italy at nineteen. She had returned from Italy and shortly after found out she was pregnant. Her family had not known, she did not tell them and they had not noticed anything. They had just assumed she had a good time in Italy, the travelling was done and she had come home to reality, to get on with her life.

It had been a terrible time, a time of utter turmoil and conflict, but she had known, deep down, she could not look after the baby alone, she did not want to. She wanted a career, a family later. She had never been sure if this had been the right decision or not, but she had learned to live with it.

She had been clever at hiding the pregnancy and had planned everything. At nearly five months pregnant, she left to work in London. The adoption had been easy to arrange, but she had not realised how quickly things would happen. She only had the baby for a few days and then she was collected by her new family and gone; she only had a small photo to remember her. She had named her Catherine, her gran's name, but she did not know if this is what she would be called now. The email blinked at her, she blinked back. *What now?* she thought.

David laid on his bed, intending to have a short nap and a bath. The latter would take him the rest of the afternoon as doing everything with one arm was tediously slow. He texted his children and messaged a few friends, including Emma, and laid down. He heard Francesca close the door and head down the steps to the terrace. He looked towards the small window and propped himself on the pillows to rest. He drifted off to sleep, thinking only briefly that he had messaged Emma but not thought to text Barbara.

Diana and Francesca gathered up a bottle of prosecco from Gianluca's not so secret stash under the table and two glasses from the kitchen, sneaking in and out like naughty school girls, and made their way to the terrace. They laid out two loungers facing the sea and settled down to sit in the sun. They toasted the day and chatted effortlessly about life at home, work and plans for the rest of the year. Francesca had plans to travel more and work less and Diana wished for the same, but knew it wouldn't happen just yet. Francesca wondered if she could tell Diana about the email. Then thought better of it, she did not know what she was going to do herself yet. Diana wondered if she could confide in Francesca. But thought better of it, she didn't know how she felt herself yet.

Chris heard the familiar noise of a message arriving. It was late and he was up too late, given he had work in a few hours, but he could not sleep. He looked at the photos of handmade gnocchi and terracotta tiled terraces with a view of the ocean with small fishing boats sailing by. He read about the coast road and how dangerous it is and how surprisingly delicious limoncello was. He also read the group were buying lottery tickets and were hoping for a big win tonight. She promised to fly him over if she won. He looked at the photo of her in a pink dress. He messaged to say he liked that dress and she quickly responded, 'Why?' He looked at her again, sunglasses, soft silky brown hair and messaged, 'Nice colour, looks good, visions of ripping it off or just leaving it on and pulling it up!' He sent a devil emoji and a wink for good measure. The message came back, 'Blimey, I will wear it more often!'

Gianluca and Rocco shared a car into Amalfi where they went their separate ways. Gianluca was shopping for dinner that night and the lesson tomorrow morning, as well as lottery tickets. The more he thought about winning, the more he wanted to win.

Gianluca visited the shops and stalls surrounding the main square and purchased fresh fruit, bread, chicken, garlic, pancetta, tomatoes, basil, risotto rice, seafood including mussels, clams and squid, courgettes and aubergines. He filled his bags quickly and took them back to the car. Rocco was making his own way back to the villa. Gianluca checked his list to make sure he had everything. He would stop on the way back to the villa to pick up wine, limoncello and the winning lottery tickets.

Rocco waited in the bar in the square, overlooked by the Cathedral of St Andrew. He watched Gianluca disappear into one of the side streets, shopping for the ingredients for meals tonight and tomorrow. He did not intend to be long; he wanted to make sure she understood once and for all. He could not see her again; this would be the last time. He sipped his beer and waited.

He watched her walk towards him, appearing from the same side street Gianluca had just entered a few minutes earlier; he wondered if Gianluca had noticed her. Her long brown hair was shining in the sunlight, perfectly straight with expensive sunglasses perched on her head and her designer bag clasped close to her side; her navy blue dress was just the right length with a zip running from V-neck to hem *Easy to take off*, he thought. Her flat tan sandals showed her perfectly manicured feet and polished toes and the colour matched her bag exactly. She was always so immaculately dressed. She smiled at him, with perfect white teeth, he smiled back. His stomach flipped. He waved to the waiter and ordered another beer and a gin and tonic. One last drink to say goodbye could not hurt.

Chapter Nine – Dinner and Lottery

Gianluca watched Francesca and Diana as they laid in the sun sipping prosecco, listening to music through their headphones. He could see Francesca looking at her phone; something appeared to be troubling her and she looked deep in thought, whilst Diana was obviously in a conversation with someone as he could hear the sounds of messages going back and forth. He wondered if it was Fleur.

He put the shopping away and stored the wine, prosecco and limoncello under the table. He covered them with a cloth and hoped the stock would last out the week, but doubted it; he knew his not so secret stash had been found.

He tidied the kitchen and dining room and then began to prep for dinner. He wondered where Rocco was, it was getting late; he had better get on with preparing the chicken ischia for dinner tonight. He cut the chicken into pieces, fried garlic and added some pancetta. He added white wine and once cooked down he added the chicken, turned the heat down and put the lid on. He would leave this for about an hour, adding vegetable stock, tomatoes, basil, seasoning and more wine.

He quartered some tomatoes and diced others, sprinkled them with salt, leaving them in a sieve to drain. He finely sliced red onions and then tossed the drained quartered tomatoes and onions together with olive oil and a little red wine vinegar.

The diced tomatoes were mixed with a little finely chopped garlic, olive oil and basil. He sliced the fresh bread and griddled them quickly, rubbing them with a fat garlic clove whilst they were still warm. He would top the cooled slices with the tomato mixture later for a starter of bruschetta. Dessert would be fresh fruit tonight, with lemon gelato.

Gianluca texted Rocco, where was he? Suzanne and Felipe had thankfully returned safely from their walk, no more trips to hospital or incident reports to complete, and it was getting late. Felipe was slightly envious of Francesca and Diana, who seemed to have enjoyed a sleepy afternoon on the terrace, rather than a long and what was likely to be a very expensive walk to a ceramics factory. He was annoyed with himself as he had forgotten to ask Gianluca to pick up a few beers for him to enjoy with dinner tonight. Although he had enjoyed a beer at a café opposite the ceramics factory earlier, he had resented the cost, ten euros for a small glass, and that had tasted more like shandy. He had sat and admired the coast line, sipping the weak beer, briefly glancing over at Suzanne who was busy choosing the table and chairs, sending photos to friends to help make the choice, or was it showing off just a little bit? Well, they could afford it, so it would be rude not to, he thought, and then chuckled to himself. He had held his beer up to Suzanne who had at that moment looked up from admiring the table she had chosen and caught his eye; she had wondered what he was up to now.

Felipe was glad to see Gianluca bring glasses to the terrace, even if it was a glass of prosecco. Suzanne was telling Diana all about the table and chairs she had seen; showing her designs and how she was confirming the purchase tomorrow on the way to Positano. Felipe thought the girls both looked very good in their swimwear, Francesca in a bikini and Diana in a black one piece reminiscent of a 1950s' film star, very elegant he thought, especially with the big sunglasses. Suzanne saw Felipe looking at Diana and Francesca; she made a mental note to keep an eye on him later.

Felipe watched Diana and Francesca leave the terrace to get ready for dinner. David had just made his way up from his room and was with Gianluca, who was helping him with buttons and adjusting his sling, and Anna was nowhere to be seen. Felipe admired the views, smiled at Suzanne and thought it was time to leave before she said anything; he would go and dress for dinner tonight.

Back in her room Francesca stared her laptop for a long time. She could not bring herself to open the email just yet. She wanted to hope for a bit longer, maybe wait until she got home to avoid disappointment on holiday. Or she could wait until after dinner tonight or maybe tomorrow. She busied herself getting ready for dinner to avoid making a decision.

Anna had enjoyed her nap and after a shower, felt refreshed. She would make her way to the terrace and read until dinner. She wondered if Gianluca had any gin, she fancied a gin and tonic on the terrace.

Suzanne joined Felipe to get ready for dinner. He was already on the balcony, having climbed through the large window. She was surprised he had made it through in his long trousers. She watched him admiring the views and felt a pang of guilt; was he enjoying himself? This holiday was her idea, after all. She picked a new pair of shorts and a tee-shirt and went to shower and change. She would join him on the balcony soon.

Diana wondered how Fleur was. She would be getting ready for the surgery tomorrow. She wanted to call or at least text, but the arrangement was to call Fleur's godmother tomorrow night for an update.

Diana still felt guilty being in Amalfi and had surprised herself by staying; it was not like her, completely out of her comfort zone. She took a deep breath and reprimanded herself; Fleur had been adamant that she stayed; there had been no question of her returning with her. Diana, after much consideration, thought this had been a wise decision by Fleur. Fleur had said from the start that if she was to get through this, she needed positivity and she set about removing herself from negative people and experiences. Withdrawing from some social circles and taking the offer from her godmother, her mother's old school friend who was a very matter of fact, no nonsense woman, to support her after the surgery. If Diana had left with her, this would have been a negative experience. Fleur was also quite wise, she knew this experience would be good for Diana, she needed to stay and complete the week on her own.

She stood at the balcony door in a towel, combing her hair through, looking out at the dark, rippling sea and the surrounding cliffs full of twinkling lights, a view she found absolutely mesmerizing and calming and one she never tired of. She was surrounded by people, but also felt very alone and thought she would love to be sharing this experience with someone; holidaying as a couple like Suzanne and Felipe. She stepped out, closed her eyes and breathed deeply, the blackness engulfing her, enjoying the silence. She stood only for a little while, holding onto the rail, before hearing a cough. She turned and looked to her left; Felipe was also enjoying the view. Diana pulled a face and went back inside. Awkward!

David stayed on the terrace; he had come up as others were going to their rooms to dress for dinner. He would read and enjoy the quiet, maybe text Barbara, he had not heard from her, actually not at all since he had been away.

Gianluca busied himself preparing the evening meal. Rocco had not returned and had not texted. He was worried; he hoped there had not been an accident on that coast road.

Rocco watched her sit down, cross her long brown, glistening legs and look at him through thick black lashes. He felt his breathing quicken and he knew she was not going to make this easy for him. In fact, she was going to make it very hard for him indeed.

Rocco looked at the time. Mamma mia! Gianluca would be fuming. He had not meant to, he had meant to say this was it, the final meeting, the final drink, the final time. He really had. But she had looked so good. He knew when she was walking towards him, she had meant to seduce him, to not let him go easily and it had worked. He was weak. A few drinks later and they had found themselves heading to a local hotel through the narrow cobbled streets, stopping to kiss, pushing each other against hard, uneven stone walls when they thought no one was looking. He had known when sipping his beer, looking at her coming towards him in the square, this would happen. He had pictured gently pulling down the zip of her dress, revealing her expensive lingerie underneath; pulling the dress from her shoulders, and letting it drop to the floor. He knew he would not resist and she had known this too as she walked towards him across the square, her eyes fixed on him. After all he thought, it would be rude not to.

Rocco hurried the cab along. *Mamma mia*, he thought, *what now?* She had watched him go as she got ready to leave the hotel. She would return to her life and he to his, for now. *Mamma mia*, he lamented, what had he done, again.

Gianluca watched Rocco rush in, apologising, but not explaining why he was late. He put on his apron and took over. Gianluca went to finish laying out the dining table; dinner was nearly ready.

Diana looked at herself in the mirror. Her black dress with gathered front was quite dressy and a bit booby and her black strappy sandals were a bit high, but she thought what the hell, they had both travelled with her to Italy and deserved a night out, and anyway, it would be rude not to. She didn't get out much.

She made her way up the two flights of stairs, carefully hoping to god she didn't slip, to the dining area, and walked through to the terrace. She was the last to arrive and she felt a bit miffed that everyone else appeared to have had a few glasses of prosecco already.

Diana picked up a glass and made her way over to Anna, who was wearing a flowing white top, adorned with sparkling blue and white sequins, and white linen trousers. Her blue eyes twinkled playfully and the sparkle from the sequins made her eyes seem bluer than ever. Diana could hear Anna saying, "Well, David, everyone's different, what a world this would be if we were all the same." Diana thought Anna enjoyed being the one who dropped little things into conversations to start a debate as you never expected her to.

Francesca looked serene in an elegant wrap, floral print, maxi dress which Diana thought she had seen her purchase in Capri; David had long trousers, but with sandals, thankfully no socks; presumably shoes were too hard to lace with one hand; Suzanne in shorts and tee-shirt; and Felipe surprisingly in stone coloured trousers and white shirt, soft shoes complimenting the chinos.

Diana felt over dressed in her black cocktail dress and heels and it did not help that Suzanne immediately pointed out that her cocktail dress was very stylish for the terrace and how did she manage to get up the stairs in those heels? Diana thought she saw Felipe give Suzanne a look and nudge her. Gianluca announced dinner was ready and the group made their way to the table. Diana sat next to Rocco, David in between her and Anna. Francesca, Suzanne and Felipe sat opposite. Diana liked to sit on this side of the table as she then had the views out of both windows and door to the sea and cliffs, a view she reminded herself nightly, she wanted to make the most of and remember always.

Rocco and Gianluca busied themselves bringing in dishes and pouring wine before joining the group at the table. On the final trip to the kitchen, Diana saw Rocco pick up the stack of lottery tickets on the side; he caught her watching him and he rolled his eyes, exclaiming loudly to the group, "Mamma mia, Diana thinks I am going to run off with the tickets." The group watched him put the tickets back on the shelf and hurry off to the kitchen. Gianluca hurried over and picked up the tickets and put them in his top shirt pocket, patting them to show the group they were safe now. It crossed Diana's mind that they could win and they would never know if Gianluca wanted to run off with the winnings; it was all in Italian after all.

The group dined on plates of bruschetta, followed by a local chicken dish, with bowls of fresh salad, all served with local wines and enjoyed with friendly conversation. The meal ended with coffees and the group decided it was time to check their lottery tickets over a glass of limoncello.

Gianluca shared out the tickets and Felipe went first. Although no one wanted to admit it, they all wanted to win and win big, something big enough to share and make a difference. Diana had visions of being interviewed on TV about how the group had won and Gianluca pictured his wedding on his super yacht, which he now had a share of rather than owned, with the group in attendance.

Felipe's ticket was a disappointment and yielded nothing. Diana could feel the tension around the table as everyone sat back in their chairs, pretending not to care. Diana's vision of a friendly group being interviewed on TV changed to a group bickering and divided over winnings and whose idea it was. *Maybe this is not a good idea after all. Maybe I should think about a syndicate contract?* Diana scolded herself in her head and reminded herself this was just a bit of fun and they were not going to win anyway. *Although it could be us. Stop it!* she shouted at herself. The group looked at her questioningly. Diana was sure she hadn't shouted that out loud and looked away quickly.

Next was Anna. She took her ticket and a euro from Felipe and began scratching off the little gold coins to reveal the five numbers to match; five numbers that could change their lives forever. Anna looked up and exclaimed she had won something and passed it to Gianluca who confirmed a win of twenty euros. Anna was very pleased. She never won anything, but then how could she; she never bought a lottery ticket at home, perhaps she should. David followed, with Francesca holding the card while he gently scratched off the gold coins first, then more quickly the wads of notes, revealing no matching numbers. Rocco walked in and stood watching from the doorway, tutting that the euros would have been better spent on food or wine or both, but stopped mid-sentence when Francesca waved her ticket excitedly. Another win of fifteen euros. Rocco took a deep breath and returned to the kitchen relieved. Maybe he should throw a few euros in the kitty if they were buying more the next day.

Diana felt nervous scratching off the grey layers; she was worrying what would happen if they won, but then reprimanded herself for worrying about something that would probably never happen. *There it is again, probably!* Scratching away at the layer covering the wad of notes revealed another win of ten euros. All hopes were now with Gianluca. Gianluca looked at the group and then his scratch card; he had not won anything. The yacht sank with an imaginary splash. With signs of disappointment Gianluca collected the winning cards, totalling forty-five euros. They all agreed to spend the winnings on more lottery tickets when they visited Positano. They would do the same again the next night upon their return to the villa.

Chapter Ten – Cooking Lesson Number 4 Before Positano

Cooking lesson number 4

Risotto Alla Pescatora – Seafood Risotto

Arborio Rice
Clams
Squid
Garlic cloves
Parsley and chili
Onion
Olive oil
Vin Santo wine and chicken stock
Salt and pepper
Tomato and Rocket salad to accompany risotto

The group met once again in the small cramped kitchen for their fourth lesson. Diana looked around the kitchen at the bowls of scary looking squid and the colander piled high with tiny pinky-grey clam shells and winced.

Rocco wasted no time and sent Francesca and Anna outside to the table to chop parsley, garlic, onion and chili. Suzanne was passed bowls of bright orange, red and yellow tomatoes of varying shapes and sizes, and a wonky cucumber, with the strict instruction to chop into small bite size chunks and put in a sieve over a bowl and sprinkle it with salt. David was put to work supervising the pans on the hob, which would soon contain the chopped garlic, onion, parsley and rice; one pan simmered with freshly made chicken stock made from the chicken dish the night before. Diana and Felipe were given the task of tapping each clam on the shelf above the sink and rinsing it; if its tiny hinged shell opened, the clam was to be discarded.

Once all these tasks had been completed, the group reassembled and Rocco demonstrated how to clean and prepare the squid. Diana watched, trying not to heave, as Rocco pulled the tentacles of the squid from the hood and cut off the tentacles just below the head/eyes, which seemed to be looking at her, begging to be released back into the sea, even though it was clearly dead. Diana remembered her first childhood holiday to Tenerife where she had been served a yellowy rice dish, something she was not used to at home, but had been willing to try. She stuck in a fork and pulled out a rubbery looking tentacle with all the sucker things, which was so unexpected that she was put off paella for many years.

Rocco placed the tentacles to one side and then a plastic looking piece was pulled from the hood and tossed in the bin. This Rocco explained, with the help of Gianluca translating a little, was the quill and should not be eaten ever and that care should be taken to avoid cutting the ink. The body was cut into rings and both body and tentacles were rinsed under running water.

In pairs, they each took turns to prepare a squid. Diana watched Suzanne and Felipe swiftly prepare the squid, with no hesitation, appearing to have done this many times, probably for their paella parties, she thought, picturing them both in front of their huge paella pans serving portions to guests with Felipe smiling and saying to anyone that would listen that it would be rude not to try. Anna and Francesca set about theirs with a methodical approach and then it was her turn. Rocco took her hand and gave her the squid, which felt wet and slippery, and she could feel her stomach churning as she pulled the tentacles from the body with what she was sure was a slurping noise. Felipe shouted, "It's alive!" and for a split second she believed him and nearly threw it. He laughed and poked her on the shoulder and said, "Got ya!" She carried on and was rather proud of herself as the finished product lay proudly on the plate, glistening from its recent wash.

The parsley, garlic, onion and chili lay sizzling in the pan, ready to receive the rice, which was tossed in and stirred until coated and transparent. Vin Santo wine was added with a sizzle and Gianluca took the rest, pouring each member a small amount in a shot glass to taste. Diana enjoyed the sweet, nutty taste and made a mental note to add this to the ever-growing list of things to buy when she got home and hunted down a nearby Italian deli.

Rocco pulled Diana to the pan and told her to stir whilst he added a ladle of stock, chastising her if she stopped, poking her and saying, "Stir, stir." He passed the ladle to Francesca and between the two of them they stirred and added stock until the rice looked creamy and, after a quick taste, was declared by Rocco as nearly ready. He tossed in the clams and a few minutes later, the squid. Gianluca returned from setting the table on the terrace and shooed everyone outside where a tray of prosecco was awaiting them. The group removed their aprons and took their seats for lunch.

Rocco and Gianluca joined them, each bringing an oversized patterned bowl, one with a salad topped with torn basil and one with the seafood risotto, which was decorated with chopped parsley and a few lemon wedges. Rocco served the risotto and the group helped themselves to side plates of salad, Gianluca topped up the prosecco and sat down, raised a glass and said, "Salute, cin cin." Diana, Suzanne and Francesca took photos of the food and the group and promised to send them on once email addresses or phone numbers, or both, had been exchanged.

Lunch over, the group retired to the terrace to relax before getting ready for their afternoon and evening in

Positano. Gianluca had left them with strict instructions to be at the top of the villa to meet the minibus and Gennaro at two-thirty p.m., so they did not have very long.

Diana had watched Gianluca leave, looking anxiously at his watch. She had wondered why. She had seen David go to his room to get ready, the first to leave as it would take him longer to get ready and walk up the steps to the top. She saw Francesca finish her glass and leave saying she would meet everyone up top; she left looking at her phone. Diana looked at Suzanne and Felipe, already ready to go, sitting quietly, looking out to sea, or at least Felipe was. Suzanne was sending messages and photos to someone, maybe her children or to her son with the café and paella parties. Diana stood up and let Anna know she was going to get her things from her room, she would see her shortly.

Chris heard the familiar ping of a message arriving, it was past midnight, but he was awake. His mind was thinking about Amalfi, a place he had not managed to visit whilst in Europe and now regretting big time. He looked at the photos of seafood risotto and a group of people enjoying lunch together on a terrace in the sunshine and again wished he too was there; he would enjoy socialising and getting to know everyone, particularly her. After years of messaging a woman he had found so attractive at twenty-nine, but had not had sex with, not even kissed, he felt he had gotten to know her just a little; they were both quite closed books. He knew he was her 'one regret', but she had been married when he met her; he did not know if she still was. He knew things could not be all that rosy and wondered what had gone wrong, maybe nothing, maybe they had just grown apart; maybe that was wishful thinking. She seemed strong, independent, caring, generous and funny and still looked great; in fact, she looked better now than all those years ago. He breathed deeply, he needed to meet her again, kiss her, make love to her. They both talked about this a lot, a road trip to Uluru in a convertible, top down. He smiled at this as he had said he couldn't wait to see her with the top down and it had taken her quite a while to realise what he meant. They had also talked about meeting in New York and meeting in Miami; he made a mental note to start saving now.

Chapter Eleven –Positano

Gennaro was waiting with the minibus. He was a small man, with shoulder length peppery grey hair and brown playful eyes. He often ferried tourists about for Gianluca, when Giovanni was not available. He enjoyed the drives between the villa and trips to Ravello, Positano and Amalfi. He enjoyed talking to people and it was good money, especially when taking Americans and lately Russians; they tipped well. He would banter with the ladies and sometimes joined the groups for dinner in the villa, when Gianluca let him and thought he would behave himself.

He watched the group make their way up the steep steps to the coast road and small courtyard where the minibus awaited. He looked at Anna who was already sitting down under the pergola; he guessed she had made a start earlier than the others, being a bit older, and then at David; he had obviously fallen already, he wondered what he had done and how he had done it. He worried for them; although beautiful, this was not an easy villa for the older person or those with difficulties walking, too many steps and stairs and lethal when it rained. He himself had slipped on the tiled steps and terraces once too often. Although one too many beers or sneaking out to avoid Gianluca, may have been the reason, rather than the rain.

Rocco was glad to see the group assemble and leave on time for their visit to Positano afternoon; he wanted the villa all to himself later.

The minibus wound its way along the coast road, cliffs to the right and wide open sea to the left. Gennaro drove with the window down and one arm resting outside, telling the group that the restaurant they just passed belonged to his family and served the very best spaghetti vongole ever. He pointed out the limoncello factory, supposedly where Jamie Oliver bought his limoncello, and the small gelateria on the right, belonging to his family, which, of course, served the best gelato in all Amalfi.

Unluckily for Felipe, the minibus pulled over outside the ceramics factory at Suzanne's request and the group disembarked. Diana, Anna and Francesca went wandering about the factory, looking at shelves displaying ceramic plates, vases, urns and much more; admiring the tables and chairs of all shapes and sizes, as well as the written orders placed from all over the world for the renowned ceramic topped tables and chairs— labelled with names like Mr and Mrs Hyde-Smith, London and Mr and Mrs Howard, Los Angeles— and Diana pictured in her mind the delivery, months after the holiday in sunny Amalfi, when it had felt like a good idea to spend thousands on a table and chairs for a patio area somewhere in windswept Britain. They viewed the many photos on the gallery wall of tables and chairs in situ with thank you notes to the factory from grateful customers. They wowed at the cost and waiting times for the exquisite handmade furniture, costing anything from a few thousand to tens of thousands of euros, and up to a year's wait for delivery, depending on the design.

They passed Suzanne and Felipe choosing their round table and four chairs, more Suzanne to be fair, with a resigned Felipe looking on, and they carried on up the stairs to another area full of ceramic plates, bowls, plaques, vases and outdoor pots and stools.

David had waited outside the factory and then decided he would like an ice cream, so crossed the road and bought one, not thinking how he was going to pay and take the cone with his one hand. Fortunately, the man serving waited, albeit a bit impatiently he thought, whilst he pulled out the euros from his pocket and placed them on the counter and then took his cone. It was delicious, but already melting and running down the cone towards his hand and arm; he could see he would need help from Gianluca to clean up in a short while. He returned to the factory and waited outside for the others, licking the ice cream furiously. Gennaro said he should have asked for his help as the ice cream shop was in his family and David wondered why he was a minibus driver as his family seemed to own most of the restaurants and cafés along one of the most famous coast roads in the world.

Suzanne and Felipe returned to the minibus, their purchase made; Suzanne was ecstatic and Felipe looked apologetic; Anna nudged Felipe and said it would be an investment and after all, it would have been rude not too. The group laughed at this as Gennaro drove on, the coast road stretching out ahead of them, the sun shining and the views magnificent.

After about twenty minutes, and without warning, the minibus suddenly pulled over and Gennaro announced the minibus could go no further and Gianluca would be leading the group the rest of the way into Positano on foot.

The group left Gennaro and the minibus and followed Gianluca. The narrow passageways between picturesque multi-coloured buildings, led the group to a small road lined on the left with railings and a beautiful view of the sea and busy seaside resort down below. The houses and villas stretched from the sea and coast below to the cliffs high above; houses in a variety of whites, beiges, terracottas and creams overlooked the sea and the busy marina where the ferry from either Amalfi or Capri was depositing and collecting their latest tourists. The view to the beach area included orange and lemon groves and deep green trees with bright red flowers. On the right the road was lined with scooters and the pavement with arching trees with intense dark pink blossom. Across the road, on the far right, houses and villas meandered up the cliffs with steep stairs edged with ceramic pots full of herbs and other dark green foliage.

Reaching a set of steps, Gianluca pointed down the path and said this would lead to the beach area, passing shops and boutiques on the way. When you reached the shops, another path, led to a walk leading up to the church/duomo at the top, which was quite steep, but once there, had lovely views. From the top you could short cut down, missing the shopping area, through another signed pathway to the beach, but it was, he warned, a way down that was quite dark and quite steep. He would meet the others at the bar on the sea front, as he would walk with Anna, avoiding the steep route, taking the gentler, but longer, route to the beach.

David decided to stay with Gianluca and Anna; he did not want to risk another fall. Suzanne, Felipe, Diana and Francesca made their way to the shops with the aim of finding the other path up towards the church, and soon found themselves in a myriad of passageways with small boutiques on either side, selling crafts, ceramics, pasta, lemons, shoes and clothes. Overhead was latticed with a wooden trellis, straining under the weight of climbing plants with the pinkest flowers Diana had ever seen. Old fashioned hanging lights adorned the walls at regular intervals and Diana thought if the lights all worked, it must be a beautiful sight at night, and wished the villa was nearer so they could walk here later. Having found the path to the duomo, they walked on, climbing higher now, the views stunning and the steep path getting a little difficult. They stopped and looked down at the shops and cafés below, winding down to the beach and where the ferries were, but could not see the church above which Gianluca had mentioned. Diana took a photo of a convertible Volkswagen Beetle in a pristine white that offered a shuttle service from a local hotel to the beach and briefly wondered if she could get a lift, but then saw Suzanne checking her steps counter, and thought better of it. After all the food and drink this week, she could do with a little exercise too.

After a while, they decided to give up trying to find the church, they must have taken a wrong turn somewhere. Luckily, they managed to spot a path with a signpost down to the beach and found themselves walking down wide, winding stone steps with a narrow channel carrying flowing water—at least they hoped it was water—running alongside. The steps meandered through ramshackle, dark buildings which looked unused, but on closer inspection were inhabited, and wandered down the dimly lit steps to the shopping area, emerging into the brightness. They carried on another path which opened out onto the beach.

The group walked out onto the seafront, which reminded Diana of Cattolica in the 1970s. A family holiday for a cousin's wedding and her first time on a plane had introduced her to Italy with its crowded beaches, bedecked with rows and rows of sunbeds, looking out to sea, all available to hire.

Positano was like a step back in time; no cabanas here, but rows of white sun loungers in front of blue and white changing huts, all very unpretentious, but somehow chic and fashionable in an iconic picture postcard setting. The huts edged an esplanade which separated the beach from the shops and cafés, with young waiters enticing passers-by to come in with the promise of the best pizza or the best pasta they had ever tasted. The beach ambled towards the ferry port and she could see sunbathers watching the ferry leaving after emptying itself of day trippers or returning guests, eager to join them on the beach or in the cafés.

Diana wondered where Gianluca meant for them to meet and looked up and down the esplanade until she spotted Anna, David and Gianluca in a local café. She waved and Anna nudged Gianluca who jumped up and came to meet them.

Anna watched the group come through the crowd and step onto the esplanade and was about to wave, when Diana spotted her. She was glad they had arrived. David was nice company, but since the Miss Marple reference, she was still unsure how he viewed her. She thought he was lonely, although she remembered he had mentioned Barbara and an Emma, so maybe loneliness was not his dilemma. She wondered why neither of them had accompanied him.

The group sat at the table, overlooking the beach, people watching; young couples hand in hand joined families laden with bags of children's toys for fun on the beach. It was busy and crowded, but it had managed to remain very Italian, despite the tourists and obvious commercialism. There were many restaurants and bars, all of which appeared very informal with plastic tables and chairs covered with white table cloths clipped down to stop them blowing away. Diana wished that the seaside resorts at home were more like this.

Gianluca ordered drinks and the waitress soon returned with a tray laden with gin and tonics and two beers, banging them down on the table and leaving rather brusquely, muttering under her breath. She returned with bowls of olives and placed them down with a thump, so hard, a few jumped out and rolled across the table. Gianluca watched the waitress walk away and kept one eye on the manager. He did not want any trouble; it had only been one date, after all

There was a little free time to wander the cobbled streets surrounding the beachfront, to the rear of the restaurant, and Diana wandered off on her own to peruse the many small eclectic shops. She strolled through a very brightly painted yellow shop selling pasta, tea towels and all sorts of things lemony, where she found an egg cup in the shape of a scooter. She collected a few things from her travels, friends, unusual cups, egg cups and wine stoppers. She thought fondly of the donkey wine stopper from Greece and the cup in the shape of a ski boot, which sat proudly on her dresser at home, providing happy memories of the children riding donkeys in Rhodes and a family ski holiday in Vermont. Then she remembered that one donkey had decided to gallop off down the steep rocky path from the acropolis and how her son had skied past her at high speed, at age seven, whilst she was on the drag lift, shouting, "Hey, Mum!" Both of which had nearly given her a heart attack.

Rocco sat at the table on the terrace outside the kitchen, looking at his watch; she was late. He had cleared away after lunch, showered and prepared a few canapes. The prosecco was on ice. His phone bleeped, she was here at last. He ran up the steps, pressing the remote to open the gate as he neared the top. He could hear the car horns honking as her taxi would be holding up the traffic on the coast road; he really should have waited for her up here.

The group met up early evening at the beachside café they were at earlier. After their saunter around the shops, each had a small bag of souvenirs. A small area had been set aside in the corner of the café at the front overlooking the beach, with glasses of prosecco and a large board laden with olives, marinated courgettes and cured meats. Diana sat down and looked out at the ocean. She had been wondering and worrying how Fleur was all day, how had the surgery gone, had it gone well? She was both looking forward to and dreading calling to find out.

The group relaxed over the prosecco and antipasti and watched the café fill up with evening diners. Gianluca disappeared to buy more lottery tickets and returned to a frosty reception from the waitress, who ignored his request for replacement beer, as she had taken his earlier glass, despite it not being empty. Diana caught his eye and he looked upwards; she guessed he had upset her on a previous occasion, she guessed the waitress had turned out not to be 'the one'.

Gianluca gathered the group for their stroll to the restaurant for their evening meal. He would not tell them much about the restaurant as he wanted it to be a surprise. Gianluca waved goodbye to the waitress, but was ignored, so he pretended to wave at the manager instead, who also ignored him. *Oh well*, he thought, *time to find another restaurant next time I visit Positano.*

The group left the beachfront café, crossed the small road and walked along the path on the right, adjacent to the beach. The path led them out alongside the beach towards the sea, and ambled up the cliff side. Night was drawing in and the lighting cast a magical pathway to the restaurant, which was set in the cliffside, overlooking the sea. Diana stopped and looked back at the beach and the hotels and houses rising above, high into the hill tops.

Large terracotta urns with pink and white flowers led walkers either to the restaurant or back to the beach. As they walked on they could see other small secluded beaches with ramshackle cafés and lounger hire. It seemed to Diana that wherever there was a beach, it was inhabited, no matter how small.

They continued along the twisting footpath, flowers spilling over the pots making it a colourful route, and as they approached the restaurant Diana could see a round window jutting out over the cliff edge and she hoped this was where their table would be. They climbed the steep, narrow steps carved from the cliffs, to the restaurant entrance with an elaborate black and gold sign welcoming them inside. The group followed Gianluca and made their way to the reserved table, which was towards the rear of the restaurant on the left-hand side and, as luck would have it—or Gianluca planning it—in the round window area jutting out over the cliff. The side of the restaurant was open and their table perched out over the sea. It was a striking view and possibly one of the nicest places to sit and eat, Diana thought, that she had ever been to.

The group settled in their seats and waiters quickly brought local wines of the region, placing bottles of red and white on the table. Plates of delicate bruschetta, squid, olives, caprese salad and cured meats followed, together with baskets of bread and dipping oils and thick red balsamic vinegar. Diana watched Suzanne and Felipe take a photo of themselves and the food as Anna checked in. She could see David looking around the restaurant at the couples and thought he looked a little sad; she saw Francesca check her emails and sigh deeply. She wondered what they thought of her; she wondered whether they ever wondered what she was thinking as she did them. She wondered if they knew she was lonely, as she looked around the restaurant at the couples enjoying each other's company.

The second course was seafood scialatielli, a traditional dish of the area, comprising of long, square sided pasta served with prawns in a garlic sauce. The main course was sea bream topped with capers and lemon slices served with bowls of salad, roasted tomatoes and green beans. Dessert was a semifreddo topped with crushed hazelnuts. Conversation flowed quietly and easily and lots of photos were taken to remember the food as well as the setting and evening overall. One of the waiters very patiently took a group photo, but had to do it several times from several phones. Diana was not sure if anyone remembered she had to call about Fleur, but then she caught Anna's eye and she knew; she knew they had all remembered, but did not want to say anything.

Diana waited for the coffees to arrive before quietly slipping away to call Fleur's godmother and find out how Fleur was after her surgery. She felt sick; what if things had not gone well, she could not bear it; she could not bear it if Fleur was suffering, it was unthinkable that she had been here having a lovely day whilst Fleur had not. She decided she would not tell the group and spoil such a wonderful day and evening. She would explain things tomorrow, but only if she had to.

She made her way to the entrance and down the steps to the path. She looked out towards the blackness of the sea and nervously dialled the number. The phone was answered almost immediately and Diana heard, "Don't worry, Diana, it's gone well and she's resting now." Diana didn't realise quite how much she had been worrying until hearing this, the relief was overwhelming, her stomach relaxed and tears welled in her eyes, she felt sick with relief.

She managed to say, "Are you sure?" and was told yes, the surgery had gone as well as it could and Fleur was already sitting up in bed with a cup of tea, her only complaint being that she had been told she could not knit for several weeks.

Diana returned to the group and passed on the good news; they were all pleased for Fleur and asked Diana to send her their very best wishes. Diana felt relieved and relaxed with her coffee and the view. She did not want to leave. She made a note to herself to do one of the new DNA tests you could order online which determined your ancestry, she was sure there would be Italian there somewhere, she felt so at home.

The group left the restaurant and strolled back to the beach front, which was surprisingly quiet. They walked past the café they were at earlier and turned right into a small, cobbled street, lined with shops, still open, restaurants and a few bars. The latter were busy and Diana wished again this place was nearer, so they could stay a while longer and walk back to the villa. She looked at Gianluca who was on the phone, she thought to Rocco.

"Change of plan," he announced. "Time for a nightcap in Positano before the minibus home."

Rocco sat looking at the room, sighing. The afternoon had started well after he had met her taxi. She looked stunning as usual and not for the first time he wondered why she was interested in him. They had sat on the terrace sipping prosecco and nibbling on olives whilst sharing memories of when they first met. She had accompanied a friend on an Italian cooking experience to this very villa last year. She was used to fine dining, designer clothes and everything that accompanied someone with money; that became obvious as the week went on. She spoke beautifully and had an ease about her that came with having money. He liked that, nothing seemed to worry her, he had thought she seemed the type of woman who always got what she wanted.

She had made it obvious she liked him from the start and they had spent a lot of that week enjoying each other's company, including the nights, before going their separate ways. They had been discreet; although he was sure the friend must have known. He had assumed he would not see her again, another holiday romance, but she had showed up this year. She had found out he was in the villa again and stayed nearby in Amalfi. She messaged him to say she wanted to see him again, that's all she said. Since then, she had messaged him and turned up at the villa unexpectedly. Fortunately when Gianluca was out, or had she planned that? Rocco knew Gianluca would not like this, he did not want any trouble or to lose his job.

Rocco wondered what would happen now. They had enjoyed sex on the terrace, something he would be reminded of for a while as his back hurt like hell and he didn't like the reminder that he was getting older. They had laid outside staring up at the sky for some time. They had chatted about going home to their own lives and he thought they had reached an understanding, that this was the end. Enjoyable while it lasted here in Amalfi, but now over. He should have known better. Things changed when he had said she had to leave as the group would be returning soon. She had accused him of getting ready for his next victim and threw a glass at him. She had finally left, but not before throwing more things at him and shouting in a very unladylike way.

Where was the ladylike finesse when he needed it. He hoped it was finally over now; he must not speak to her or see her again, no matter how good she looked. He must not give in.

Gianluca worried what had happened, was there damage to the villa? This would not go down well with the company or the owners. He did not want to lose this job over Rocco and one of his 'friends'. He enjoyed the hosting experience, he was good at it and it was only a few months of the year, perfect for him, particularly now as he wanted to return home to Sicily and settle down. Perhaps invest in a small boutique hotel where he could offer private cooking lessons.

The group had sat down in one of the many bars on route to meet the minibus, outside under a pergola struggling under the weight of exuberant pink trailing flowers. Gianluca had let Gennaro know about the unexpected change of plan, who he knew would not be happy about the delay.

The air was thick with the smell of flowers and lemons which seemed to be growing in every available pot and space. Felipe and David were enjoying a beer whilst the ladies had opted for gin and tonics; all agreed it was a welcome change from prosecco, as much as they liked it. Gianluca had enjoyed hosting for this group; they were easy going, undemanding and no complaining, even from David, who had every reason to complain, given his shoulder and how and when it had happened.

Gianluca reached for his mobile to call Gennaro to arrange to meet and return to the villa and felt the lottery tickets; he had forgotten about them. He rapped on the table and pulled out the tickets, waving them at Diana. The group looked up and realised what he meant. He could see their expressions change as each began to think about what they would spend their winnings on. He had already moored his shared super yacht in the nearby marina and later would make his way to the bar on the beach to meet Stefania, who he then pictured having words with the waitress. Stop, go back, make his way to the restaurant on the cliffs instead.

Gianluca handed out the tickets and one at a time, each began the ritual of rubbing off the little grey covering to reveal the answers, looking to match the numbers. Cards done and handed back to Gianluca for checking, revealed only thirty euros won tonight. The initial excitement of playing the lottery was wearing off with the daily disappointment. The group decided as there was only one day left, they may as well pool their winnings one last time and play again for a final time tomorrow night at their farewell dinner. Gianluca went to pay the bar bill and the group agreed in his absence, that any winnings from tomorrow night's tickets would be a tip for Gianluca, unless it was the jackpot of course.

The group met a grumpy, silent Gennaro and travelled back to the villa, planning to meet in the middle lounge for a nightcap of limoncello. Gianluca hoped his supplies would last out; there was only one more evening after all.

Diana watched Positano disappear into the night and sighed, looking at the houses, bars and cafés en route to the villa. She would have liked to stay in Positano and return back to the villa later. If she had one complaint about this holiday, it was that the villa was remote. No late night trips to local restaurants and bars, there was nothing nearby and cabs were too expensive; walking on the coast road in the dark was not safe, especially after a few limoncellos.

Chris was becoming increasingly impatient for the messages from Italy to arrive, although the latest photo had made him think. The group photo at a table overlooking the sea was causing him to feel uneasy. He thought she looked lonely, and the guy sitting opposite her was looking quite intensely at her rather than at whoever was taking the photo. Then there was the young guy sitting next to her, he was good looking and he probably thought her easy pickings, a sugar mummy. Stop it, he almost shouted at himself, stop being ridiculous. Jealous of a photo and at his age. He looked again; she should not be alone in Italy, in a restaurant overlooking the sea. She should be wined and dined in that restaurant, in the company of someone who loved her and wanted to be with her, who would take her back to the villa and make love to her on that balcony overlooking the sea, with dolphins swimming by. Oh my god, he thought, since when had he become a romantic, he was a rugby player for god's sake.

Chapter Twelve – Yet More Limoncello

Gianluca took a tray of limoncello and glasses to the middle lounge and opened the doors to the terraces. He had scanned the rooms briefly and could not see any problems, but could not find Rocco, who had made himself scarce, so he would have to talk to him tomorrow. He put some music on low and went out to the terrace. He looked out at the sea and thought about going home to Sicily, Catania. A few more weeks here in Amalfi, one more cooking group followed by a Pilates group, and then he would be home. He was looking forward to seeing his family and friends, it had been too long.

Rocco heard the group returning, but stayed in his room. He had cleared up and left things tidy. Gianluca would not find anything out of place, other than a few missing glasses. He was going to bed, his back was hurting and his phone was off, Mamma mia, what a day.

The group reconvened in the middle lounge and chatted briefly about their trip to Positano. Suzanne had her iPad and Diana suggested a quiz to end the evening. Suzanne quickly found a quiz online and offered to be quizmaster, asking general knowledge and trivia to the group as a whole. David and Anna sat together and Felipe made a point of sitting between Francesca and Diana, cheerfully announcing to anyone that would listen, "That it would be rude not to join in and he was a thorn between two roses," His positioning did not go unnoticed by Suzanne and Diana saw her raise her eyebrow at Felipe and give him a look as if he were a naughty child. A look that clearly said, 'I'm watching you'.

The quiz was a huge success, but not taken seriously, with no winners or losers. Like children, Diana thought, happy to take part. They sat together, talking effortlessly about the day and finding out more about each other. They all had further travel plans except Diana. Diana questioned when had she stopped planning holidays? There was a time when she had three or four holidays a year, plus short breaks. But these had become less and less in recent years; planning to suit everyone had become just too hard.

Diana talked about her parents who had been married for fifty-five years, and how her mum had been ill for some time. She recounted the latest hospital admission with a smile and explained the reason for this smile was when a young doctor had asked her mum how she and her husband got on at home. Her mum had misunderstood the meaning of the question, answering, "Fine, he's in one room and I'm in the other."

Felipe said he wanted to travel more, but was waiting for Suzanne to retire so they could travel the world with rucksacks together. David said he was thinking of moving nearer to his daughter and her family when he returned home. Anna asked if his partner would be joining him, but he said he thought not.

Anna said she had booked to return to Amalfi later in the year and would be enjoying a visit from her son who lived in Australia soon, which she was really looking forward to.

Francesca said she had a holiday with her husband planned for a few weeks' time and was hoping to progress in her job and travel more with the company who had offices in America. She was looking forward to seeing her dogs and her husband at the weekend. Suzanne said she would think about retiring as she had always wanted to visit Miami and asked Felipe if this was on his list of destinations.

As the limoncello came to an end, so did the evening. It crossed Diana's mind that Gianluca would not be happy that they had gone through another bottle as he would have to buy another for the last night, unless he already had one in his not so secret store under the table. Diana wondered if Gianluca preferred the Pilates weeks; they were probably healthier eaters and drank less and didn't cost so much in limoncello and maybe just the odd bottle of prosecco.

Diana went to the kitchen and made a weak milky coffee and took it to her room. She changed and took the drink out onto the balcony, sitting in her chair, looking out to sea, sighing at the thought of only one day left; only one more cooking lesson. She heard a noise and looked around, Felipe waved from his window and mouthed goodnight. She nodded and smiled and returned to gaze at the sea, wondering how on earth she was going to find the courage to leave here and return to normal life, whatever that was.

Chapter Thirteen – The Last Day

Diana awoke early to the sun once again streaming in through the balcony doors. She looked out to sea and watched the birds fly past several times before getting up. She grabbed a hairbrush and went out onto the balcony, brushing her hair as she went, feeling the heat from the sun on her head and neck as she did so. She stood looking out to sea for some time, looking for answers; looking for a sign to tell her what she should do.

Diana returned to her room and set about packing, leaving out only what she would need for the day and tomorrow morning. She hated packing; packing to go home always felt worse, but was easier to do. Worse because you were at the end of your holiday; easier because you could just throw it all in without worrying, just wrap anything fragile and liquids in bags. Everything would be washed anyway. It did not take long and she was ready to leave the room sooner than she thought. She grabbed her phone and apron and wandered along the corridor to the conservatory and out onto the terrace. Looking out over the balcony to the large pizza oven below, she noted that it had been cleaned and there was a very large stack of freshly cut logs to the left of it.

She walked along the terrace to the balcony overlooking the small pool below and made her way up the steep stone steps to the terrace which met the breakfast room and kitchen. She was the first to arrive and made her way to the kitchen, where she could hear Gianluca and Rocco. Gianluca pointed to the coffee pot on the stove and passed her a mug. Diana took the coffee and went outside to the terrace, thinking she had got far too used to this, very quickly, and how much she missed the sunshine and being outside at home. Coffee in a cold, back garden in North London with grey skies was not quite the same.

Their final cooking lesson would be after breakfast and Gianluca seemed excited; he said he had a surprise for the group this evening.

Diana was soon joined by Anna and Francesca and the three of them sat quietly on the terrace, sipping their fresh coffee. Diana would miss this, the company, the views and quickly looked away. She must enjoy today without feeling sad as it would all be over too quickly. Diana was glad it was sunny on the final day; this afternoon was free time, so a bit of sunbathing before the evening's activities, whatever they were to be.

Diana enjoyed the last of the lemon marmalade, but did not miss Gianluca's' concerned look. She reassured him that he did not have to buy any more for tomorrow, his budget was safe. Over breakfast Gianluca explained that as he and Rocco were from Sicily, they wanted the group to enjoy preparing typical Sicilian dishes of arancini balls and veal meatballs. These would be eaten with saffron risotto and salad.

Sicilian Arancini and Sicilian Veal Meatballs

Arancini:

- 10 1/2 ounces Carnaroli rice
- pinch of saffron mixed with 2 tablespoons warm water
- 1 cup chicken stock (more may be needed)
- 1 cup white wine
- 4 shallots, finely chopped
- Olive Oil
- 2 fat cloves of garlic
- salt and pepper
- breadcrumbs
- vegetable oil for frying

Veal Meatballs:

- 1lb minced veal (or more depending on the number of meatballs needed)
- fresh breadcrumbs
- 2 cloves of garlic, minced
- 1 tablespoon Parmesan cheese
- 1 teaspoon chopped thyme
- salt and pepper

- zest of one lemon
- lemon leaves
- olive oil
- cocktail sticks

The group assembled at the table on the terrace, which was laden with the bowls of ingredients for the last time. Rocco quickly assigned tasks as usual. Diana to chop shallots, Felipe to chop garlic, Suzanne to measure the rice, which Rocco explained was carnaroli, "The king of risotto rice." But, if you could not get this at home, as he was sure they couldn't, to use arborio. "Never use rice without a high starch content," he scolded. "You will never get the rich creamy texture if you use the wrong rice," he tutted, adding, "Mamma mia!" to make his point further. Anna measured out the white wine which she hoped would be served with lunch, too, as it was a particularly good one, and Francesca mixed a pinch of saffron with warm water.

The group followed Rocco to the kitchen where a large paella type pan was on the stove. He splashed in oil and the shallots and garlic, and sautéed both until opaque, then added the rice, making sure all the grains were tossed in with the mixture of onion and garlic. Next to the pan was a large pot of simmering chicken stock. He took the white wine, measured by Anna, and poured that into the pan. Rocco beckoned Gianluca for the remaining bottle and splashed in a bit more white wine, stirring all the time. He called Diana and Felipe, Diana to constantly stir the risotto whilst Felipe added a ladle of stock at regular intervals. Rocco added the saffron to the rice, together with salt and pepper, indicating with hand gestures to keep stirring. When the stock had all but gone, he gave everyone a teaspoon and asked them to try the risotto. The verdict was a little more salt and it was done. Rocco removed the large pan of risotto from the stove and placed it to one side, to cool completely before attempting to make the arancini balls.

Whilst the risotto cooled, the group returned to the terrace to make lemon and veal meatballs, a traditional Sicilian dish.

Each had a bowl to mix minced veal, breadcrumbs, minced garlic, Parmesan cheese, chopped thyme, salt, pepper and the zest of a lemon. The group had fun shaping the mixture into balls the size of walnuts and then wrapping them in a lemon leaf, securing each meatball with a cocktail stick. They looked very pretty and would be brushed with olive oil and roasted in the oven.

The group washed up and made their way to the terrace. Gianluca had left a tray of prosecco for their break, whilst he and Rocco cleared the table and prepared for the next part of the lesson.

Chris was well engrossed now. He had always wanted to know how to make a risotto, a favourite of his, although he would have to add chicken. What was a meal without meat? He watched the brief video and again wished he was there. She always involved him when she travelled, joking she was taking him with her, and he would ask, where are we going this time? He would ask for a sexy location shot and she would send him a photo, but it was always with the title, view from my sunbed. He lost count of the number of photos of her legs he had received over the years, albeit very nice legs.

He looked at the video again. The group appeared to be getting on so well, given they had not known each other long. The views were stunning, but she was there alone and he was here alone, what should he do, carry on with this chatting or find out once and for all, was she his destiny or not? They joked and flirted with each other and they appeared to have things in common, but was it real? She had been married, when they had met, and there had been no indication this had changed. He had never asked her and she never asked him about women, only joked, 'I hope you are behaving yourself'. She had said his wedding photos were lovely and that he had looked so handsome. She had sent messages when his wife was ill and asked if she could do anything or help in any way. But she never asked if he was divorced, never asked if he was seeing someone and he did not ask her, he did not want to know, so he guessed it was the same for her.

Diana sipped her prosecco and listened to the group making their plans for next week, plans she was no part of. She had no plans; she was not sure what she was going to do, other than leave this villa.

Back at the table, there was a large bowl of cooled risotto, together with a bowl of flour, whisked eggs and breadcrumbs. Rocco and Gianluca demonstrated shaping the cooled risotto mixture into a pear shape, rolling it in flour, dipping in egg and then breadcrumbs. These, they explained, were the typical shape and would be sold all over Sicily as a typical street food. They could be stuffed with cheese or ragout, before coating, and were deep fried for best results. The group could choose to make balls or the pear shape, all of which would be chilled for half an hour before frying. There was much laughter as everyone tried to shape the mixture Sicilian style and Rocco and Gianluca helped to ensure the end result was edible.

Whilst the arancini were chilling, the group helped Rocco and Gianluca to clear up and prepare two salads; orange and fennel and tomato, both sprinkled with a pinch of salt and pepper and drizzled with olive oil. Diana marvelled at the variety of vivid colours, shapes and sizes of the tomatoes and wished these were available at home; She also noted the bag of fresh baguettes in the kitchen and wondered when Rocco had gone out to get them.

The group took off their aprons and adjourned to the terrace to wait for lunch to be served. Diana went back to her room and shook out her apron over the balcony. She carefully folded it up and left it on the chair for later. Gianluca had not told them what the plan was for tonight yet, but they would need their aprons once last time. She changed into her swimming costume and put a light dress on over the top. She gathered her bag with a book, headphones, sun cream, etcetera, and took this with her. She would stay on the terrace after lunch and enjoy the last few hours of sunshine. It was raining at home as usual, so she may as well lie in the sun while she could.

While they waited for lunch Diana, Suzanne and Felipe chatted about family, hobbies and travelling. Anna joined them and said she was thinking of retiring this year; although working part time was ideal, having to travel in the school holidays was not. Francesca said she had decisions to make which included whether or not to take a position abroad, albeit temporarily. Her company had offered her a secondment to New York for one year, working in Manhattan, all expenses paid. The group could not see her dilemma, what was there to decide? She did not tell them her decision would be determined by events that had happened a long time ago.

Suzanne said she would consider retiring, but would not like to do nothing. She liked to keep busy so she would need to focus on something she wanted to do like helping her son in his café or doing something with photography. She loved taking photos and videos and sharing these with all her friends and family, some of whom lived on the other side of the world.

Lunch was delicious and everyone enjoyed sharing the platters of arancini, salads and meatballs. Rocco had cooked a tomato sauce to accompany the meatballs and there was also saffron risotto. Dessert was a success too, being a slice of cake that Rocco had made. He explained his orange cake was a Sicilian dessert, one his mother used to make, and made using all of the orange, peel included. Diana made a mental note to find this recipe when she got home, as it was lovely and something different to make rather than her usual lemon drizzle.

Lunch over, everyone went their separate ways for the afternoon. Diana made her way to the sunbed on the terrace and settled down with her earphones and a glass of prosecco. Suzanne and Felipe donned their rucksacks and left for a walk, assuring Gianluca they would take care on the roads, and Felipe laughing they had a few thousand steps to make up for so who knows what time they would be back.

David went to pack, knowing it would take him longer than everyone else. He also planned to ask someone to meet him at the airport as he would need someone to drive him and his car home. He suddenly remembered that Barbara has not responded to an earlier message.

Anna went to pack and for an afternoon nap. She opened her windows wider and let the gentle breeze flow in. Looking out to sea, she thought how she thoroughly enjoyed these breaks and was already looking forward to the next one in October. She wondered what the group would be like; she hoped it would be mixed, always more enjoyable when it was not just all women. One of her groups had included a Pilates group and she had complained to the travel company on her return, as really, cooking and Pilates? They just did not mix. The Pilates group had also been friends travelling together, meeting the same instructor again, so it had been quite uncomfortable at times. They had not been foodies, no interest in cooking or what they ate at all, and complained about the trips too; complained about a lot, come to think of it. She had been fortunate there was another couple enjoying the cooking and the husband had been quite a wine connoisseur, an added bonus as he had made sure there was always a decent wine on the table for lunch and dinner. She liked this group, no fuss, no complaining, no uncomfortableness. She hoped for the same in October.

Francesca looked at her emails, in particular the one she had not yet read. It was strange to think this may determine her future. She opened the email and there it was. Her daughter wished to make contact; she had been looking for her after all. *What now?* Francesca was relieved and overwhelmingly scared at the same time. *What now?* Now, she would go home, tell her husband and take it from there. He would need to be involved in anything she wanted to do next. *Oh well*, she thought, *I've done it now. Bloody internet makes it all too easy to arrange cooking holidays on a whim and find long lost daughters.* She thought it would take longer, thought it would not be this easy; she thought she would have more time to come to terms with her decision to find her.

Sitting on the terrace, listening to music, was relaxing. Diana sipped her prosecco and looked at the turquoise sea, watching the boats that passed by every now and then. She enjoyed the warm glow of the sun and feeling warm from the inside, although she was not sure if this was down to the sun or the prosecco. Her mind was racing, veering wildly from staying in Amalfi and working in a trattoria as a waitress to leaving on a plane from Naples to anywhere else but London. She often felt sad at the end of holidays, but this time she felt different. She contemplated briefly asking Gianluca for help finding a job or if he knew of anything; If only she could win the lottery, this would take the financial and practical worries away and she would just have to concentrate on her emotional ones. She hoped Gianluca had purchased some winning tickets for tonight.

Diana must have dozed off as she woke to the sounds of voices in the kitchen and Gianluca calling to someone on the terrace below. She sat up and looked around. She hoped she had not been snoring or worse, dribbling.

Gianluca called Diana, to hurry, lesson in an hour on the terrace below, pizza making with a chef from a local pizzeria. Diana thought he seemed very excited about this and decided that he must love pizza. She gathered her things and made her way to her room to get ready.

Diana made her way down the terracotta tiled steps to the terrace below. The pizza oven was built into the space adjacent to the stairs and the cliff, with an elaborate brick chimney consisting of zig zagged bricks rising into a point. The oven was fired up and full of burning wood; tables had been assembled and the one to the side of the oven seemed to be buckling under the weight of bowls of cubed mozzarella, tomatoes, tomato sauce, roasted courgettes, basil and bottles of olive oil and balsamic vinegar. A large oblong container held plump looking dough balls, cotton wool soft and pale in colour. This Diana assumed, was the pizza dough, all ready for pizza making.

Propped against the oven were two long handled shovels, which Diana guessed were to put the wood and pizza deep into the hot oven to cook. As she was thinking about this, a man dressed in casual clothes with a black apron and black headscarf, threw more wood into the oven, shouting to someone on the terrace about it, it seemed he needed more wood.

Luigi was the chef for the night, visiting from a local pizzeria in Amalfi. He did not speak much

English, so Gianluca was on hand to translate. With Gianluca's help, Luigi explained that each person would take a turn at rolling out the dough, layering with toppings of choice and putting the pizza into the oven. Luigi tossed the dough, spinning it effortlessly in the air, making a small plump mound grow into a misshapen disc, almost see-through. He topped the base with two ladles of the tomato sauce, sprinkled with cubed mozzarella and basil and scooped the base onto the shovel and deposited it into the oven with ease. The key, he explained through Gianluca, to authentic Italian pizzas, is to keep them simple and have a thin base.

Anna was first, pushing the dough out with her palm and turning. She tossed it in the air and Luigi caught it to the relief of Anna and much laughter from her friends, all of whom thought this was obviously going to happen to them too. Anna topped her dough with the tomato sauce, mozzarella and courgette. She was handed the pizza shovel, which was taller than her and with one very quick scoop, and huge sighs from the group, the pizza was on the shovel. She turned and deposited the pizza into the hot oven.

Luigi stepped forward and pushed Anna's pizza further in and pulled out the one he had made earlier, from the oven, already bubbling and crisp. He flipped the pizza from the shovel to the board on the table, put the shovel to one side and picked up more basil which he tore and scattered over the pizza. He drizzled it with olive oil and cut the pizza into slices, indicating for the group to help themselves. Luigi pulled Anna's pizza from the oven and drizzled it with olive oil, sliced it and shouted, "Salute, salute!"

The pizzas were delicious and possibly the best Diana had ever tasted. Thin and crispy every time from now on. Next it was Francesca's turn, followed by Suzanne. Both completed their pizza and oven deposits effortlessly, which was intimidating for the next person, which happened to be Felipe. Felipe winked at Diana and said, "Difficult to follow that but, oh well, it would be rude not to have a go," and set about forming a pizza. The first flip went well but the second not so much and Luigi did not manage to catch the dough, being distracted with a beer, and it landed with a splat on the terrace amidst Rocco shouting, "Mamma mia! Mamma mia!" Felipe made his second pizza with a token flip, eyeing Rocco as he did so, and topped it with sauce and courgettes, asking where the pineapple was, which set Rocco off once more.

Felipe helped David to produce a pizza and then it was Diana's turn. Diana always found it difficult to take part in things when she had to do something in front of people, but had decided to try, despite her nerves. Something nearly always went wrong or not to plan, like the time she took the kids on a husky ride whilst skiing and was the only one to capsize, or the horse riding where she had what appeared to be the biggest horse in the world and was the only one to bolt. She fully expected to drop the dough and burn the pizza, but hey ho, like Felipe, she thought it would be rude not to give it a go.

Surprisingly for Diana, the only thing she found difficult was picking up the huge shovel and trying to get the pizza on it. But with a little help from Rocco, this was soon resolved and her pizza topped with sauce, sautéed onions and mushrooms was soon bubbling in the oven. Anna pointed out that a local supermarket at home had last year sold pizza oven kits for the back garden and if they did so again this year, she would certainly consider it.

There were so many pizzas to eat, Diana wondered if they would get through them. A table was set laden with the recently prepared pizzas and bowls of salads, looking resplendent in the evening light with the soft candles burning.

Diana thought it was strange that they had been in the villa for one week but this was the first time on this terrace and wondered were there other nooks and crannies she had not found? This was a magnificent villa, albeit quite remote and probably not the same in the winter months. She wondered how the owner, allegedly one old lady, lived here alone.

Rocco brought a typical Italian ice cream, stracciatella for dessert which he explained was vanilla ice cream with tiny flakes of crunchy chocolate as well as the best ice cream in the world, according to Rocco, gelato from Sicily which was flavoured with jasmine and did not contain eggs. There was also a bowl of granita, which Rocco insisted they try as this too was from his Sicilian home.

The evening was a great success and a fitting end to the week, although tinged with some sadness for Diana, as it was the last evening the group would spend together. Tomorrow morning would be the drive back to Naples airport and goodbyes. Diana always disliked goodbyes, finding them awkward; she hoped this would not be the case tomorrow.

Gianluca came to the terrace with a tray containing one final bottle of limoncello, an array of small glasses and several lottery tickets. He poured out the limoncello and began to pass out the glasses, the first to Diana who he now called limoncello lady. He raised a glass to the group and said salute and thanked everyone for a wonderful week and how he hoped to see them all again on another holiday. Luca had a few more hosting holidays before returning to Sicily later in the summer and then he was off to the Antarctic later in the year.

The group had one final go at winning the lottery, scratching off the little grey areas, sending tiny bits flying off into the night. Sadly, the winnings were minimal and the group agreed to give the winning tickets to Gianluca, together with a tip, tomorrow morning.

Chris saw the familiar red dot meaning there was a message and picked up his phone. He read the message and read it again, she was not going home; she was getting a flight from Naples to Sydney, would he meet her? He couldn't believe it. He messaged for flight details and to say of course he would meet her, he couldn't wait. He added, it had been far too long and would she be wearing the pink dress he had liked so much?

Suzanne looked at Felipe after messaging and felt sorry for him. He had no idea what was planned for tomorrow. Anna wondered what surprise Suzanne had in store for her husband, she guessed something was up from the look on Suzanne's face after messaging, it was a look of I hope I've done the right thing, whilst she looked at Felipe.

Francesca sat quietly within the group, sipping her prosecco, sighing a little. This was going to go one way or the other with her husband; she hoped he would understand her decision not to tell him about her daughter and the decision to find her. Coming to Italy this time had for some reason brought back some very happy as well as upsetting memories and had resulted in her long-awaited attempt to find her daughter, an attempt which had proved more successful than she had ever anticipated. She hoped that all would work out, if not, there was always New York.

Diana felt quite sick and this was not due to the limoncello. She did not feel right, but then she never wanted to go home at the end of a holiday, she had always found it hard returning to normality and the stresses and strains of everyday life.

David was worried, he had not heard anything from Barbara and was wondering how he was going to get home from the airport. He would have to text his daughters, perhaps they could help.

Rocco tidied the kitchen and put away the crockery for the final time this week. He collected up his equipment, packing it into a box and bag to take to his next destination which would be home, for the time being. Another cookery course was scheduled for next month, but this time in Sicily in a local villa, no travelling, he could go home at night. He hoped to god she did not turn up there. *Mamma mia*, he thought, what if she did, the wife and father-in-law would not be happy.

The group said their goodbyes and adjourned to their rooms. David finished packing as he was finding it difficult with one arm; Suzanne and Felipe went to bed as their rucksacks were packed; Francesca checked her emails and looked once again at the information confirming that her daughter was looking for her. She would do no more until she had spoken to her husband; she hoped it was not too late to involve him.

Anna closed the door for another week and sighed. She had really enjoyed this group, she hoped to stay in touch with a few; she would like to know how their plans made this week turned out.

Diana looked out to sea on the balcony with a glass of prosecco. She watched the moonlight dance on the sea and listened to the lapping waves whilst she thought about her decisions. She hoped her children would understand, they were older after all.

Chapter Fourteen – Going Home

The last morning dawned and the group sat quietly eating breakfast before taking their bags and cases up the steps to the top terrace. Rocco and Gianluca followed the group to say their goodbyes and were surprised when Felipe thanked them on behalf of the group, for a wonderful week and gave them both a tip from the group. The group took up their usual seats in the minibus and settled in for their final ride with Giovanni, the trip back to Naples. The journey was quiet and felt too quick to Diana. She wanted to savour the view and lock them into her memory.

At the airport, Francesca said her goodbyes as she was heading back to Rome for one night and then home from there. David said farewell too, and the remaining group watched him struggle with a trolley using his one good arm to steer his way rather hurriedly through the crowd towards his Manchester flight, seemingly oblivious to the people he bumped into on the way. David was in a hurry to get home now. His plea for help to meet him at the airport and drive him home had been answered not by his children, nor Barbara, but by Emma. She was meeting him and driving him home and he had laughed when she had said 'it would be rude not to'. He would have to explain why when he saw her, as well as why he had taken so long to decide she was the right one for him.

Suzanne and Felipe left quickly for their flights to the Channel Islands, no luggage to check in, only rucksacks, Felipe pointed out with glee, no queuing for him.

Anna and Diana made their way through security after check in and sat down together in the bar in the departures lounge. They enjoyed one final prosecco together before making their way to their respective flights. Anna hugged Diana and wished her well; she hoped to see her back in London soon.

Diana sat on the plane; it felt like a long journey ahead. She felt anxious about the decisions she had made, but it was done now, there was no going back. It was a relief not to be in limbo any more. She slept and ate and was relieved when the plane finally landed. She made her way through security and then went to the ladies before collecting her suitcase. She changed her top, pinched her pale cheeks, brushed her hair, brushed her teeth and dabbed some perfume from a small travel bottle Fleur had given her. She took one final look in the mirror and made her way through the doors to the arrivals area.

Suzanne sat on the plane and hoped it would not be delayed; they had a connecting flight to catch. She had ordered a bottle of champagne and was going to tell Felipe she had made arrangements to retire and had booked a trip for them to America at the end of term. They were going to drive Route 66—something Felipe had always wanted to do—and there was no return date. They could do what they liked, when they liked and for how long they liked. She hoped he would enjoy the surprise; he had been nagging her to retire long enough.

Diana scanned the crowds in arrivals at Sydney International Airport and it took some seconds for her to spot it: there amongst a sea of people greeting their loved ones and chauffeurs and drivers with typed signs to meet and greet, was a huge handmade sign. It read 'Hey, hot stuff'. Diana walked towards the sign and to Chris; they stood looking at each other for what seemed like an eternity. Diana stood unable to move as she looked at Chris and watched him drop the sign and put his strong arms around her, enveloping her, holding her close. She sighed; she finally felt safe and where she belonged.

Chris looked at Diana and could not quite believe she was here. He stepped forward and put his arms around her, squeezing her tightly, crushing her body against his. He could feel her breathing heavily and knew she was anxious; anxious about the decisions she had made. He cupped her face and kissed her, their first kiss. It was hot, passionate and very intense. Someone walked past and they both heard them say, "Get a room,

168

guys," and Chris knew finally, in that moment, she was his destiny, they had to try for a future together, they had wasted too much time already, and anyway, it would be rude not to.

Printed in Great Britain
by Amazon

84895549R10099